THEY TOUC____ __

"Do you like the restaurant?" asked Sir Thomas.

"Very much, thank you."

"To you, my dearest!" he murmured, raising his glass with a smile.

Temia followed suit and took a sip from her glass.

"Is it to your taste?"

"It's most delicious, Sir Thomas, but can we order something to eat?" asked Temia, taking another sip. "I shall get a headache if I drink this without food."

He snapped his fingers and a waiter appeared.

"Two *steak entrecôte*, please," he ordered.

Temia and Sir Thomas chatted away until the food arrived and then, she drank some more champagne.

As she set it down, she noticed there was something sparkling in the bottom of her glass.

"Oh, what can it be?" she said, picking it up and examining it.

"I thought you would never notice, my love!"

Temia dipped her finger into the liquid and pulled out a diamond ring.

"Oh!" she cried, holding it up to the light.

"Yes, my darling. I want you to marry me. Temia, will you? I love you so very much and want nothing more than to spend the rest of my life with you."

THE BARBARA CARTLAND
PINK COLLECTION

Titles in this series

1. The Cross Of Love
2. Love In The Highlands
3. Love Finds The Way
4. The Castle Of Love
5. Love Is Triumphant
6. Stars In The Sky
7. The Ship Of Love
8. A Dangerous Disguise
9. Love Became Theirs
10. Love Drives In
11. Sailing To Love
12. The Star Of Love
13. Music Is The Soul Of Love
14. Love In The East
15. Theirs To Eternity
16. A Paradise On Earth
17. Love Wins In Berlin
18. In Search Of Love
19. Love Rescues Rosanna
20. A Heart In Heaven
21. The House Of Happiness
22. Royalty Defeated By Love
23. The White Witch
24. They Sought Love
25. Love Is The Reason For Living
26. They Found Their Way To Heaven
27. Learning To Love
28. Journey To Happiness
29. A Kiss In The Desert
30. The Heart Of Love
31. The Richness Of Love
32. For Ever And Ever
33. An Unexpected Love
34. Saved By An Angel
35. Touching The Stars
36. Seeking Love
37. Journey To Love
38. The Importance Of Love
39. Love By The Lake
40. A Dream Come True
41. The King Without A Heart
42. The Waters Of Love
43. Danger To The Duke
44. A Perfect Way To Heaven
45. Follow Your Heart
46. In Hiding
47. Rivals For Love
48. A Kiss From The Heart
49. Lovers In London
50. This Way To Heaven
51. A Princess Prays
52. Mine For Ever
53. The Earl's Revenge
54. Love At The Tower
55. Ruled By Love
56. Love Came From Heaven
57. Love And Apollo
58. The Keys Of Love
59. A Castle Of Dreams
60. A Battle Of Brains
61. A Change Of Hearts
62. It Is Love
63. The Triumph Of Love
64. Wanted – A Royal Wife
65. A Kiss Of Love
66. To Heaven With Love
67. Pray For Love
68. The Marquis Is Trapped
69. Hide And Seek For Love
70. Hiding From Love
71. A Teacher Of Love
72. Money Or Love
73. The Revelation Is Love
74. The Tree Of Love
75. The Magnificent Marquis
76. The Castle
77. The Gates Of Paradise
78. A Lucky Star
79. A Heaven On Earth
80. The Healing Hand
81. A Virgin Bride
82. The Trail To Love
83. A Royal Love Match
84. A Steeplechase For Love
85. Love At Last
86. Search For A Wife
87. Secret Love
88. A Miracle Of Love
89. Love And The Clans
90. A Shooting Star
91. The Winning Post Is Love
92. They Touched Heaven

THEY TOUCHED HEAVEN

BARBARA CARTLAND

Barbaracartland.com Ltd

Printed and bound in Great Britain
by Mimeo of Huntingdon, Cambridgeshire.

THE BARBARA CARTLAND PINK COLLECTION

Dame Barbara Cartland is still regarded as the most prolific bestselling author in the history of the world.

In her lifetime she was frequently in the Guinness Book of Records for writing more books than any other living author.

Her most amazing literary feat was to double her output from 10 books a year to over 20 books a year when she was 77 to meet the huge demand.

She went on writing continuously at this rate for 20 years and wrote her very last book at the age of 97, thus completing an incredible 400 books between the ages of 77 and 97.

Her publishers finally could not keep up with this phenomenal output, so at her death in 2000 she left behind an amazing 160 unpublished manuscripts, something that no other author has ever achieved.

Barbara's son, Ian McCorquodale, together with his daughter Iona, felt that it was their sacred duty to publish all these titles for Barbara's millions of admirers all over the world who so love her wonderful romances.

So in 2004 they started publishing the 160 brand new Barbara Cartlands as *The Barbara Cartland Pink Collection*, as Barbara's favourite colour was always pink – and yet more pink!

The Barbara Cartland Pink Collection is published monthly exclusively by Barbaracartland.com and the books are numbered in sequence from 1 to 160.

Enjoy receiving a brand new Barbara Cartland book each month by taking out an annual subscription to the Pink Collection, or purchase the books individually.

The Pink Collection is available from the Barbara Cartland website www.barbaracartland.com via mail order and through all good bookshops.

In addition Ian and Iona are proud to announce that The Barbara Cartland Pink Collection is now available in ebook format as from Valentine's Day 2011.

For more information, please contact us at:

Barbaracartland.com Ltd.
Camfield Place
Hatfield
Hertfordshire AL9 6JE
United Kingdom

Telephone: +44 (0)1707 642629
Fax: +44 (0)1707 663041
Email: info@barbaracartland.com

THE LATE DAME BARBARA CARTLAND

Barbara Cartland who sadly died in May 2000 at the age of nearly 99 was the world's most famous romantic novelist who wrote 723 books in her lifetime with worldwide sales of over 1 billion copies and her books were translated into 36 different languages.

As well as romantic novels, she wrote historical biographies, 6 autobiographies, theatrical plays, books of advice on life, love, vitamins and cookery. She also found time to be a political speaker and television and radio personality.

She wrote her first book at the age of 21 and this was called *Jigsaw*. It became an immediate bestseller and sold 100,000 copies in hardback and was translated into 6 different languages. She wrote continuously throughout her life, writing bestsellers for an astonishing 76 years. Her books have always been immensely popular in the United States, where in 1976 her current books were at numbers 1 & 2 in the B. Dalton bestsellers list, a feat never achieved before or since by any author.

Barbara Cartland became a legend in her own lifetime and will be best remembered for her wonderful romantic novels, so loved by her millions of readers throughout the world.

Her books will always be treasured for their moral message, her pure and innocent heroines, her good looking and dashing heroes and above all her belief that the power of love is more important than anything else in everyone's life.

"Everything and anything is possible when you are in love – even touching Heaven. I should know because I have touched Heaven too."

Barbara Cartland

CHAPTER ONE
1860

"You will take that back at once, de Lamerie!"

The Earl of Wentworth glowered across the green card table as he slammed down his glass of brandy on the rosewood surface.

The Frenchman stayed impassive. He was a proud scion of ancient noble Huguenot blood whose family had not escaped the tyranny of a Catholic France to be dictated to by a mere English Lord.

He merely shrugged his shoulders in an irritating fashion and pursed his lips.

"I will not – it is very clear to me that these cards are marked," he answered sardonically.

The Earl's handsome face grew crimson under his black hair and his dark eyes flashed dangerously.

On the other side of the table, his best friend, Sir Thomas Babbington set down his cards and spoke softly,

"Come now, Wentworth. There has obviously been some misunderstanding. I think all the Comte is trying to say is that he would like a new deck."

He laid his hand on the Earl's arm to restrain him as he could see that his friend's temper was near to flashpoint.

The Earl was as fiery as Sir Thomas was placid and they compensated for each other's shortcomings.

What the Earl lacked in restraint, he made up for in artistic ability. His paintings were lauded everywhere and he wrote sensitive and thoughtful verse.

"Oh, you Englishmen, you cannot shoulder a mere criticism without taking offence!" spat Comte de Lamerie, dismissively. "It's I who should be upset – you are clearly cheating and then you attempt to put the blame on me!"

The Earl arose like a striking python from his chair, as Sir Thomas tried at once to diffuse the situation.

"Come, gentlemen. Let's leave the game and have another drink. There's a fine Armagnac we've yet to try."

The Comte's face took on a sour expression.

"You are asking me to back down? Pah! Never!"

He slumped back in his chair and clutched his cards close to his chest, muttering something in French under his breath that the Earl evidently understood.

"Take that back, you blasted Frenchie!" he shouted. "I didn't spend a year in France to be oblivious to your tawdry insults!"

"Then it's a great pity you did not learn more from us," drawled the Comte, "where are your famous English manners and sense of fair play?"

That was enough to incense the Earl, as he leapt over the table and grabbed the Comte by his cravat.

"You damned Frenchie dog!" he howled, his eyes level with the Comte's.

"Wentworth! Please!" pleaded Sir Thomas.

"He has – insulted me for the last time!" choked the Comte, attempting to prise the Earl's vice-like grip away from his neck.

"Richard!"

Sir Thomas was beside himself.

He had often seen his friend lose his temper and, since his father had died last year, he had been even more volatile than ever.

The Earl's hands were curiously large and square, not at all the hands of a gentleman and they would not have disgraced a field labourer.

Sir Thomas knew that he was strong enough to kill the effete Comte with them and was terrified that one day it might happen.

Spluttering, the Comte regained his composure and drew himself up to his full height of five foot seven.

"Sir, I challenge you to a duel! We shall settle this in the French manner – with swords!"

"As you wish!" muttered the Earl in a tone that was truly bloodcurdling.

The Comte rose from his chair and then ordered the waiter to bring their cloaks.

*

An hour later the two men stood facing each other in the depths of Hyde Park.

The Comte had sent his manservant to his house for swords, but he had returned with two pistols.

He then furiously flew into a long stream of angry French while the Earl and Sir Thomas looked on.

"You have the advantage, Wentworth," whispered Sir Thomas. "He is notoriously near-sighted and couldn't hit a bull chained to a tree!"

"I will kill the blighter," fumed the Earl, clenching and unclenching his fists.

He had stripped down to his shirt and, in his haste, had ripped off the top few buttons.

His breast heaved as he tried to steady his nerves.

He knew that a shaking hand was as good as signing his own death warrant.

The Comte stood in his shirtsleeves, examining his pistol and was weighing it in his hand when a shout came up from some nearby bushes.

"*Stop!*"

Both men froze as they saw a Policeman coming towards them.

"Stop!" he shouted again.

The Comte thrust his pistol into his waistcoat just before the Policeman drew level with them.

"Sir?" he began, looking straight at the Comte.

"*Je ne parle pas anglais,*" he sneered.

"Officer, perhaps I can explain," said Sir Thomas, coming forward and quickly handing the Earl his cloak so that he could conceal the pistol.

"It was a quarrel over nothing and it has now been settled. We will be on our way at once."

"Just a moment Mr. – "

"Sir Thomas Babbington."

"I'm sorry, sir, but I'm going to have to report the incident."

"Surely, there is no need for that? It was a private matter – amongst gentlemen."

The Policeman stared at him and then at the Earl.

"You know the law, sir. Duels is strictly forbidden. Her Majesty saw to that twenty years ago!"

"Officer, there was no duel. These gentlemen were merely having a difference of opinion."

"And you assure me, sir, you will take your friend home right now?"

"At once."

"Then, I'll bid you goodnight, sir, but you mark my words, if I catch you in the Park again with pistols, then I'll have no alternative but to arrest you all, whoever you be."

"Thanks, good night, Officer. Let's go, Richard."

The Earl threw the Comte a hate-filled look and wrapped himself in his cloak.

As he turned to leave, the Comte muttered,

"*Lâche!*" just loud enough for him to hear.

"Go to hell!" answered the Earl, bridling with fury.

It was only the firm touch of his friend on his arm that restrained him.

"You should not rise to every insult that's thrown your way," advised Sir Thomas, as they ran to their waiting carriage. "It's imperative that you control your temper, Richard. One day it will prove your undoing. We are very lucky that the Officer stopped us and let us off with a caution as it could have gone badly for you otherwise."

"I have faith enough in my own ability to shoot to kill, Thomas," he answered, glowering darkly.

"And too much confidence in the lack of ability on the Comte's part. He may yet have surprised us and I don't want your mother grieving over your corpse!"

Climbing in and throwing his athletic frame into the seat, the Earl turned his face to the window as the carriage sped off into the night.

"I should have killed the bounder," he muttered, as they made their way through the damp streets of Mayfair. "And I will, if he ever crosses my path again!"

*

On the dark Southern approach road into London, a solitary carriage made its way towards the Capital.

Inside a very tired Temia Brandon and her mother, Lady Brandon, were sleeping.

Temia had spent the last few years at a Finishing School in Paris and had now returned that very day.

Her mother had been forced to meet her from the ferry alone, as her husband, Sir Arthur Brandon, was busy with his horses.

The stables at Bovendon Hall were justly famous and people came from far and wide to buy the handsome animals bred there.

Lady Brandon had waited for hours for the ferry to dock, and, when it did, she hardly recognised the elegant young lady who walked down the gangplank towards her.

"Temia! Is that really you?" she called, marvelling at her daughter's sophisticated hairstyle and clothes.

"Mama!" she exclaimed, hurrying towards her.

Lady Brandon embraced Temia and kissed her soft cheek. She smelled as delicious as she looked – a faint odour of vervain and rose wafted from her.

"My darling. Welcome home!"

"Where is Papa? Is he with the horses?"

Lady Brandon laughed, almost girlishly.

"Naturally. I need never worry about your father straying very far from home – no, my only rivals for his affections have four legs and not two!"

"Oh, Mama! I have had such a wonderful time in France. I almost feel more French than English."

"You must not let your father hear you say that, dearest. He is so proud to be British and a subject of Her Majesty, Queen Victoria."

"You must tell me all the news," said Temia, as she swept a tawny blonde curl from the corner of her mouth.

Her blue eyes were the colour of cornflowers and her striking face was sweetly heart-shaped.

It had been a windy crossing and Temia was proud that, unlike so many passengers, she had not been seasick.

The wind still blew across the quayside and made chill an otherwise crisp and fine autumn day.

"Wait until we get into the carriage," said Lady Brandon, signalling to their coachman. "We have a long journey ahead us and will be staying tonight with Cousin Georgiana and Aunt Marianne in Kensington."

"It will be lovely to see her after so long," replied Temia, climbing into the jet-black brougham.

"We will only be there overnight and before we go home to Bovendon Hall, I had hoped that we should be able to visit Jasper's memorial."

At the mention of her dead son's name, her eyes filled with tears.

Jasper had fallen at Scutari in the Crimea some five years earlier and the family had plunged themselves into a long state of mourning. Indeed, Bovendon Hall became known as the 'vale of tears' locally.

None mourned more deeply than Lady Brandon and although he had been buried in the Crimea, the family had raised a memorial for him in the churchyard at Bovendon.

*

A huge lurch of the carriage awoke Temia with a start as it jolted over a pothole. Rubbing her eyes she attempted to peer out of the window.

They were nearing the outskirts of the Capital and the roads were becoming more densely lined with houses.

As they turned towards Kensington, a carriage that was racing like the devil was on its tail came towards them and sped off towards Mayfair.

'Goodness! They are in a hurry!' she thought.

Ten minutes later, at the crossroads at Kensington, their carriage came to a halt.

Temia looked out of the window and saw a large theatre set back from the road and, although it was almost midnight, the streets outside were still dotted with people.

A crowd of girls stood giggling on the pavement along with a few gentlemen in top hats and Temia noticed a board that read,

"Tonight – *Les Jolies Mademoiselles*."

At the front of the building, the name *Royal Kent Theatre* was emblazoned in ornate silver letters.

She watched as the girls acted as if they had not a care in the world. They seemed very gay in their bright Indian shawls and fashionable bonnets.

'Show girls!' she smiled, a little excitedly.

In Paris she was aware of the *demi-monde* that was inhabited by glamorous actresses and artists. The girls in her class had whispered of nothing else and of the many scandalous goings-on in the theatres of the City.

Lady Brandon yawned and turned to Temia,

"Where are we?" she asked a little sleepily.

"I think we are almost there, Mama. Look, there is the *Royal Kent Theatre*."

She paused for a second before enquiring,

"Mama, who are *Les Jolies Mademoiselles*?"

"I hear they are the toast of London, although I don't really concern myself with such matters. They sing and dance and have been known to entertain at the very best house parties. Mainly to an audience of gentlemen – "

Her voice trailed away.

"But, Mama, you suggest they are not ladies?"

"No woman on the stage can count herself equal to a lady, Temia. Did they not teach you that at the Finishing School?"

Temia did not answer.

She liked the sound of *Les Jolies Mademoiselles* as they reminded her of Paris. She thought that Mama would have been shocked had she known that she had dined only the week before at a fashionable Parisian house where a company of actresses had sung and danced for everyone.

"Besides," added her mother, "I have some good news for you. Your father has decided to hold a ball to celebrate your homecoming and we have invited everyone we know!"

"Oh, Mama! Thank you!" cried Temia, thinking excitedly of the new ball gowns she had purchased in Paris. She had been wondering how she could justify the expense and now she had the perfect excuse!

"We shall be employing a French chef for the event and there will be an orchestra. Your father has spared no expense, as he is so happy to have you home again. You must promise not leave us again for a very long time."

"Of course, Mama!" replied Temia, waiting as the coachman climbed down to let them out of the carriage.

She thought for a moment and then suggested,

"Mama, might we have *Les Jolies Mademoiselles* at the party? If they are as fashionable as you say, then a turn from them would certainly be applauded."

Her mother froze for a moment.

"Your father would never allow such women in the house!"

Temia sensed that there was more to this remark than mere comment.

9

The light was still on in her aunt's house and then the next moment, the door was open and two footmen and a butler were soon by her side, supervising her luggage.

"Good evening, Lady Brandon, Miss Brandon. Her Ladyship will receive you in the drawing room."

"Oh, silly Marianne!" cried Lady Brandon. "Did I not write and say don't wait up as we might be very late?"

Even so, Lady Brandon and Temia went into the house and were immediately shown into an elegant room.

A small woman wrapped up in a dressing gown was waiting for them by the fire and Temia immediately ran towards her Aunt Marianne.

"Temia! Why, you have grown incredibly tall and beautiful!" she exclaimed, kissing her on the cheek.

"Thank you, Aunt. I am very glad to be back in England, but I shall miss my friends a great deal."

"Paris is a beautiful City, is it not?"

"Very," replied Temia, sitting down by the fire.

"I expect Georgiana will wish to hear everything about it in the morning. I am afraid she went to bed early with a headache. She is very sorry she could not stay up."

"How is Georgiana?"

"She is well and as grown up as you are! There is but a year between you, you will recall."

Temia laughed.

"Yes, of course. She is, I believe, twenty-two?"

"Next month and you are twenty-two at the end of the summer?"

"Yes," said Temia, "and it was such a pity to turn twenty-one and not be in England. However Papa is giving a ball for me and I do hope you will be able to come?"

"The invitations have just arrived," answered Aunt Marianne. "Georgiana cannot wait – she says she is bored with all the London gentlemen and is looking forward to meeting a good country Lord!"

"I am afraid that we are somewhat lacking in titled Lords, Marianne," came in Lady Brandon. "I have sent invitations poste chaise to Lord Wentworth and the Duke of Northampton, but not heard a word from either."

"The Duke of Northampton is very old, is he not? I cannot imagine our daughters wanting to limp around the dance floor with him. What of Wentworth?"

"Something of an unknown quantity. He has not been in the County for long. He lives in London and has only just taken up residence at Yardley Manor. His father, the old Earl, died only last year."

"Then, he will still be in mourning – "

"I could not say. In any case I am so tired that if I don't go to my bed now, you may have to carry me!"

"You must forgive me, but I am so excited to see you both. It's a pity you cannot stay for longer."

"We must return home as soon as we can. Arthur dislikes being on his own."

Aunt Marianne's butler showed them to their rooms and made certain they were comfortable.

*

Temia fell asleep almost at once and slept, deep in dreams, until the maid woke her at eight o'clock.

"Good morning, miss," she said, putting a tray on the bedside table. "Shall I open your curtains?"

"Yes, please. I hope the sun is shining! It will be a miserable journey back to Northamptonshire if it's not."

The maid pulled back the curtains and a thin beam of sunlight illuminated the room.

Temia sat up in bed drinking a cup of tea.

She mused again about *Les Jolies Mademoiselles* and how great it would be for them to perform at her ball.

'It's a pity Papa is so set against it. It would have given the evening a truly French air that I would love.'

By the time she had got up and the maid had helped her dress, she was looking forward to seeing Georgiana.

As soon as she entered the breakfast room and saw her, she could no longer contain her excitement.

"Georgiana!" she cried, rushing over to her cousin and kissing her cheek. "How lovely you look!"

"I was about to say the same thing to you as well, dearest!" she replied.

Georgiana was pale and blonde with such enormous brown eyes.

"How long can it be since we last saw each other?"

"It was the year before you went to Paris, but I did not think it possible that you should have grown so much!"

"It's an illusion, I am no taller than I was then."

"Then, it must be your gown and your hair – so *very* Continental!"

Temia blushed with pleasure and smoothed down the silk skirt of her dress. It was one of her favourites and echoed the colour of her eyes.

Georgiana ushered Temia to a chair at the table.

"And so, after breakfast, you must tell me all your news. It's a pity that you are leaving after luncheon."

"But I will see you at the ball, Georgiana?"

"Most definitely, but we shall not be staying longer than overnight. Maybe you can visit London again soon?"

"That would be lovely, but first I want to reacquaint myself with Bovendon Hall before I go rushing off again."

After breakfast Georgiana and Temia went to the morning room to view Georgiana's latest sketches.

"These are very good," said Temia appreciatively, as she took out a portfolio of animals. "How well you have captured the likeness of your little dog!"

Georgiana's King Charles Cavalier spaniel, Bob, was sitting with his head on his paws by a fireplace. He looked pleadingly up at his Mistress in the hope of a titbit.

"He's adorable, isn't he?"

"Very, although I must admit I prefer horses. I am looking forward to seeing new ones at Papa's stables."

"What began as a hobby has become a thriving business, Mama says – "

"Yes, although, as you well know, Papa is first and foremost a gentleman."

"Naturally," said Georgiana. "And he will want to make up for lost time by showing you off at this ball."

Temia laughed.

"Yes, he will and, for myself, I am pleased that I will now not have to hide the huge trunk full of gowns that I purchased in Paris!"

"You know Uncle Arthur cannot deny you a thing," replied Georgiana, putting away her portfolio.

"That is *not* quite so," answered Temia.

"Why do you say that? If it is within his power to grant you, then you know your Papa will do so."

"There is one thing he will not. Georgiana, are you familiar with the *Royal Kent Theatre*?"

"The one at the crossroads?"

"Yes, the very same. On our way here last night, I saw that there is a singing and dancing troupe called *Les Jolies Mademoiselles*. Mama says they are the toast of London and if they were to perform at my ball – "

Georgiana looked shocked.

"Temia!" she gasped, "do you know what kind of women these are?"

"Mama expressed much the same sentiment. She said Papa would never allow them in our house! In France women such as they are feted, not frowned on. Really, the English are so prudish sometimes."

Georgiana picked up Bob and walked over to the sofa with him. She appeared to be deep in thought.

"No, dearest, it's not that – "

"Then, what is it?"

Georgiana bit her lip.

"I don't know if I should tell you."

Temia looked intrigued.

"Dearest, now that you have said it – you must!"

"Very well, but you must not speak of this to your parents, as your Mama will be mortified if she thinks that I have told you."

"Georgiana!" cried Temia in exasperation.

"Promise me you won't be shocked, but – there's a rumour in the family that Uncle Arthur, your Papa, was once involved in a scandal with a dancer. It was before he met your Mama, of course. There – I have said it!"

Temia sat down with her mind whirling.

What Georgiana had just told her, stunned her.

She had always thought of her father as being rather staid and dull. Of course, he was her own dear Papa, but she could not imagine him chatting easily with those girls she had seen outside the theatre yesterday or behaving in any way less than a gentlemanly manner!

"Goodness!" she breathed. "I can scarcely believe it. I have never heard this story before."

"It's not something that's talked about. I am afraid I don't know details, Temia, and you must not say I have told you or Mama would be furious with me. But you do see why you could never have *Les Jolies Mademoiselles* set foot inside Bovendon Hall."

For the rest of the day Temia was curiously quiet and withdrawn.

Although she wanted to consider herself a worldly woman, she knew nothing of love or its darker side.

'I must find out more about this family secret,' she reflected, as they sat down to luncheon. 'But how can I discover the truth without upsetting Mama?'

And before they had started their pudding, she had resolved to get to the bottom of the matter.

'I cannot let this lie,' she murmured to herself, as she finished her plate of apple tart. 'I simply cannot!'

CHAPTER TWO

Temia did not enjoy the revelations about her father that had been a family secret for so many years.

She asked Georgiana to go over the story time and time again and then she searched for new clues.

"Are you certain you don't know any more?" she whispered, as they walked around the garden.

"I have told you everything that I know," replied Georgiana, now feeling sorry she had mentioned the topic. "All I can say is that it was before your parents married."

Temia felt frustrated.

She could hardly ask Mama what had happened in case it upset her and cross-questioning Papa was out of the question.

"There must be an old servant who was at The Hall when it occurred, perhaps Robert our groom, who has been at Bovendon Hall since he was a stable boy.

But how to broach the subject with a hired hand?

She knew it was beneath her dignity to scrabble around for titbits amongst the servants and if her Mama found out, she would be furious.

She was still pondering her conundrum when the butler informed her that the carriage was ready to leave.

*

"Temia! My darling! How wonderful you look!"

Temia ran at once to the library where she knew her father would be, the moment she set foot in the house.

"Papa! I have missed you so much!" she cried, as he kissed her cheek and embraced her.

"You have grown so beautiful, my darling. I can hardly believe I have produced such a charming creature."

Temia laughed and stroked the lapel of his jacket.

"Papa, you do yourself an injustice, you are most distinguished and wise and those virtues far outweigh mere skin-deep features."

"Well, your Mama thought so! And when I had hair, I could pass muster in a good suit and a silk hat."

"Papa, did you have many sweethearts before you met Mama?"

Temia could not believe she had had the nerve to say such a thing.

She felt her father pull away from her.

"You have been in France too long, my dear," he said, with a shocked look. "I can see that."

"Oh, I am sorry, Papa. I did not mean to offend!"

"I am not offended, Temia, merely shocked at your forwardness. You must remember that you are in England now and you must not ask such very personal questions of people. What passes for idle conversation in France is not the done thing in England."

Temia blushed.

It was true – she had become very bold in the two years she had been in Paris. There was something about the open and frank nature of the French that had struck a chord within her and she soon dropped her English reserve.

In fact, she had always been pleased if someone had mistaken her for a French girl rather than English.

She spoke French with an impeccable accent and had learnt a little Italian as well and some people refused to believe that she was anything other than Continental.

"Now, Temia, would you excuse me? I have some paperwork to finish before dinner. And I am sure a certain four-legged friend of yours would welcome a visit!"

"Lightning! Oh, how could I forget him? Papa, I must run to the stables at once!"

She quickly turned and headed for the stables.

'All seems unchanged since I was last here,' she thought with a degree of satisfaction, as she ran towards the squat building that lay some distance from the house.

The first person she saw was Robert, the old groom.

His hands were as gnarled as his face and the black cap on his head covered a bald pate. He was busy hacking at the upturned hoof of a pony she had not seen before.

"Robert!" she called across the courtyard.

"Miss Temia! You've come back to us at last!"

"Yes, I have and this time I will be staying."

"It does me good to 'ear that, miss. Lightning has sure missed you!"

"Where is he, Robert? I would love to see him."

"He's over there in yon field, you just call 'im and 'e'll come!"

Temia could not contain her excitement as she ran to the edge of the field. The proud chestnut stallion was peacefully cropping the grass but, as soon as she called, he lifted his big head and snorted.

Within moments, he had galloped over to where she stood. Delightedly, he nuzzled her hand.

"Sorry, boy. No sugar. Let me look at you!"

Lightning shook his head as if in disappointment.

"Oh, come," crooned Temia, "tomorrow we shall go for a nice long ride and you can have all the treats you could wish for. I don't want Robert accusing me of trying to make you fat and lazy, do I?"

She stroked his silky mane lovingly.

None of the horses she had ridden in Paris had been so handsome and on the rare opportunity she did have to ride, she had not enjoyed it as much as if she had been on the back of Lightning.

He had been hers since he was a foal and she had chosen him herself. He had a white flash on his nose and his father had been a champion racehorse.

As she made a fuss of him, she noticed that Robert had joined her by the fence.

"We've a new stallion in the stables, miss. Your father'll want to show 'im off to you tomorrow."

"Where is he?"

"In 'is stall. Would you like to see 'im?"

Temia paused. It occurred to her that perhaps her Papa would want to show him to her first and she did not wish to spoil it for him.

"No, I will wait until tomorrow, Robert. I must get back to the house and supervise my things. I expect that Sarah is spinning like a top!"

Robert laughed and touched his cap.

"I'll be seeing you tomorrow, miss."

"Yes, indeed," she answered happily.

Nothing could please her more than the prospect of a cross-country gallop.

*

Temia was in for a surprise when she finally went upstairs to her bedroom.

The dusty-looking wallpaper had been replaced by a far more sophisticated wallcovering and new pink silk curtains hung from the window and there was also a huge walnut wardrobe with a number of drawers.

"Oh, it's beautiful!" she gasped as she walked in.

"Welcome home, Miss Temia!" exclaimed Sarah, bobbing a curtsy. "We've all missed you."

"Did Mama redecorate the room?"

"Yes, miss. She spent months with the decorator, choosing all the colours and then she ordered the wardrobe from London. What do you think of it, now?"

"I think it's lovely. I am so glad that Mama bought me a new wardrobe – I was worried I would not be able to squeeze all my new gowns into that old one!"

"Are they from Paris, miss?"

"Yes, they are and I want you to press the burgundy silk one for tonight. I wish to make myself as attractive as possible for Papa."

The maid curtsied and left the room.

Temia peeped into her bathroom and noticed that it all seemed clean and neat with flowers in a little vase.

It made her feel welcome and glad to be home.

She looked at the small rack of books she had left there before going to France.

'These seem so childish now,' she thought, picking up Charles Lamb's *Tales from Shakespeare*. 'After reading Voltaire, I feel the need to improve my mind further.'

Temia suddenly felt terribly tired from her journey and so she lay down on the bed and closed her eyes.

It felt as if she had only been asleep for ten minutes when Sarah was by her side calling her,

"Wake up, miss! I need to dress you for dinner!"

"What time is it, Sarah?"

"It is just gone seven o'clock. You've been asleep for over an hour!"

Sarah helped her into the burgundy silk dress and then set about dressing her hair and Temia had to show her how she liked it to be done in the new French style.

Fortunately Sarah was a swift learner and Temia was soon viewing herself appreciatively in the pier glass.

"Well done, Sarah," she praised her.

"You look lovely, miss," sighed Sarah, as she stood back to admire her handiwork.

Temia smiled.

Her blue eyes sparkled and her fair hair seemed full of golden highlights in the glow of the candles. The sun was just setting and already the room was full of shadows.

Then came the very familiar sound of the gong and Temia laughed to herself.

'It's been a long time since I heard that sound,' she murmured, rising to leave the room.

Downstairs Temia could hear that her parents were already in the dining room.

"Good evening, miss!" Ridley, the butler, intoned.

"Darling. You look incredibly lovely!" exclaimed her Mama. "Doesn't she, Arthur?"

"What do you think, Papa?" she asked him shyly, displaying the skirt of her gown.

"Did I pay for that?" he asked with a wry smile.

"Yes, Papa."

"And should I ask how much it cost me?"

"No, Papa!"

Sir Arthur smiled to himself indulgently. As if he could refuse his only daughter anything!

"I hope you will not be bored in the country?"

"Heavens no, Papa," she answered, sitting down. "I missed Bovendon more than you will know!"

"You have been to the stables naturally?"

"Yes, to see Lightning! Robert tells me you have a fine new stallion?"

Her father chuckled.

"Yes indeed, I am very proud of Brutus!"

"Why did you call him Brutus? I hope he doesn't betray you in the way that Roman Senator did Caesar!"

"Because he is such a huge brute of an animal, the name seemed appropriate."

"Will you take him hunting?"

"Perhaps after I have ridden him a few times, but it's too soon. It's a pity as there's a meet this weekend."

Temia's Mama began to laugh.

"I can tell that, if I am not careful, I am not going to be able to change the topic of conversation too easily," she remarked with a sigh.

"It's a pity you don't care for the Hunt, Mama," said Temia, taking a sip of wine. "I would so enjoy us going out as a family."

"And then who would stay behind to supervise the meals? No, I prefer to stay at home organising suitable nourishment for the tired Huntsmen!"

"And women," corrected Temia.

"As you have not had a chance to ride Lightning for ages, perhaps you would care to join me tomorrow when I take Brutus out for a canter?" suggested her father.

"Oh, yes! I would love that," agreed Temia. "I so long to ride Lightning again."

"Then, it's settled. I shall ask Robert to make them ready for half-past ten and then we shall ride to the river and back. We will return for luncheon and you can tell me what you think of my latest purchase."

Temia was so excited that she could barely contain herself. The next day could not come soon enough for her.

"And the ball, Mama. Is it to be at the weekend?"

"Yes, dearest. Tomorrow I will show you the menu and we can then discuss the band. Signor Duttini will not disappoint you. He comes from Italy. The Italians have a certain flair, I always think."

"Mama, I do believe that you are just the tiniest bit in love with Signor Duttini!" teased Temia. "Papa, you shall have to be on your guard on the evening of the ball!"

"I just have eyes for the one man, Temia. Twenty-seven years we have been married and not a day goes by when I do not thank the Good Lord for allowing me to be such a fortunate woman."

"You were younger than me when you met Papa, were you not?"

"Yes, I was barely twenty."

"I am in no hurry to marry," admitted Temia. "I want to marry for love when the time comes and it must be a perfect love, like yours and Papa's."

Temia could have sworn that at very that moment, something like a shadow crossed her mother's face, but it was so fleeting that no sooner than she thought she had glimpsed it, it disappeared.

*

Temia stayed up for as long as she could, but soon her eyes grew heavy and she could think of nothing but climbing into her bed.

Kissing her parents goodnight, she went upstairs and, after Sarah had undressed her, she jumped into bed.

But downstairs in the drawing room, the scene was very different –

"You did not tell her about Lord Alphonse, then," muttered Lady Brandon, sipping her brandy sparingly.

"It did not seem the right time, Alice," answered Sir Arthur, staring into the fire as the embers died down.

"We must broach the subject sooner or later."

"What – that her father is being made a fool of by a man who has no compunction in taking the moral high ground when there is none to be taken?"

"He cannot continue taking horses and not paying for them. There is the expense and he insists on having the best. Heaven only knows how long you will be able to keep Brutus once he sets eyes on him."

"He cannot have Brutus!" grated Sir Arthur.

"But he has already made comments that he would like Lightning."

"If the time does come, we shall have to consider it carefully," he sighed, "we cannot afford to rock the boat with him too much, Alice. He is such a loose cannon and I cannot be certain he will not reveal – *a certain matter.*"

At the mention of that, Lady Brandon began to cry.

"Why are we being made to pay for something that is ancient history?" she sobbed, dabbing at her eyes.

Sir Arthur went over to her and put his arm around his wife in an attempt to comfort her.

"Is it not enough that we lost our only son?"

"Men such as he have no morals, dearest," said Sir Arthur, his face setting into a steely mask.

But even as he comforted her, he knew that Lord Alphonse was not about to disappear in a puff of smoke, no matter how dearly he wished it.

*

Next morning, Temia could not wait for breakfast to finish so that she could run out to the stables.

Lightning was waiting for her and she gave him a sugar lump as Robert saddled up Brutus for her father.

Sir Arthur came striding out, looking very dapper in his riding habit.

"I promised you he was a fine beast, Temia," he boasted, as he mounted Brutus proudly.

"He is indeed, Papa. He looks as if he is rather spirited. Perhaps, too much so for me!"

"I would not let anyone else ride him, Temia," said Sir Arthur, grimly contemplating the dreadful prospect of Lord Alphonse attempting to lay claim to him.

"He is feisty, that much is for certain. This is only the third time that I have taken him out for a long ride, so we shall see if he behaves himself."

They were soon striking out across the countryside.

Autumn was already showing itself in the hints of red that touched the trees and bushes and Temia thought that it would not be long before there were no leaves and their branches would be bare.

They chatted easily in between gallops and, as they reached the river and stopped for a rest, Temia suddenly seized on the idea of mentioning *Les Jolies Mademoiselles* to her father.

"Papa, this ball we are holding – would it not be wonderful if we had some really fanciful entertainment?"

"You mean, apart from Signor Duttini's orchestra? What would you like, dearest? If it is within my power to grant it, you know I will."

Temia took a deep breath and looked away, so as to appear as casual as possible.

"Well, I noticed when we were in Kensington that there was a dance troupe playing that Mama said were the toast of London – "

Her father stared at her with an expression that told Temia that he was a little perturbed.

"A dance troupe? Do you mean *showgirls*?"

Temia took a deep breath.

'If he becomes angry, then I will know that there is something behind this story!' she said to herself.

"Yes, in France they are not frowned upon as they are here and it might add a Continental flavour to the – "

"Out of the question!" interrupted her father with a face like thunder. "I can see that being in France for so long has warped your sense of what is socially acceptable."

And with that, he turned Brutus away from the river and galloped off in the direction of The Hall.

'Well!' said Temia to herself, a little startled. 'I did not expect such a strong reaction to my suggestion. I can only conclude there is indeed something in Georgiana's theory about a family secret lurking beneath all this!'

As she spurred Lightning into action, she could not help but be even more intrigued.

'I will get to the bottom of this,' she determined, as she crossed the fallow fields. 'There is obviously more to my Papa than meets the eye!'

*

The day of the ball arrived and Bovendon Hall was a hive of activity. Almost before dawn, the servants were making ready and extra servants had been engaged from a London agency to swell their ranks.

Lady Brandon rose early as the first grey streaks of dawn were breaking the sky, as her maid helped her dress.

"Hurry, Martha. The champagne will be here soon. The Master has had it shipped in especially from France."

"Cook is upset that you have employed a French chef to create some dishes for the buffet, my Lady."

"Cook should be glad of the help, Martha."

Mrs. Duff had been employed at Bovendon Hall for many years and was not getting any younger and although she was able to manage day-to-day menus, Lady Brandon had doubted her ability to cater for so many guests.

"Oh, I expect she does really, my Lady," answered Martha. "She must be nearly sixty if she's a day."

"Even so, we don't want to deliberately upset her, Martha. I shall have words with her later to reassure her that her position is safe until she wants to retire."

Lady Brandon did not wish for any trouble with the servants on today of all days – had she not already enough to deal with?

Temia offered to help as she came in for breakfast, but was told to relax and not worry.

But before she knew it, it was time to change.

Sarah laced her into her new ball gown from Paris and between them they devised an ornate hairstyle that Temia hoped would be a sensation.

"I don't believe you could look any more beautiful if you tried!" gasped Sarah, as Temia stood in front of the mirror in her mauve-silk gown with a frilled underskirt. The bodice was daringly low with gathered short sleeves and she wore a pair of mauve-silk slippers to match.

"You will have every gentleman in the ballroom wanting to dance with you, miss," sighed Sarah, as she did up the diamond necklace around Temia's slender throat.

She could not wait to go down and greet her guests.

And, as she did so, her mother was waiting for her with a rather cross look on her face.

"Rather bad news, I am afraid, darling. The Earl of Wentworth has sent his apologies, as he has been detained in London and cannot come. He is one of the County's most eligible bachelors – if a little wild."

"How so, Mama?"

"He is much given to the pursuit of pleasure and it is a sinful waste of talent. The man paints exquisitely and speaks several languages. I am certain that given the right woman, he would be a reformed character – there is no bad blood there, just a fiery temper, if gossip is to be believed."

"That is a pity, as I should have liked to have met him," replied Temia, taking the glass of champagne that the footman offered her. "He sounds intriguing."

Lady Brandon's eyes filled with tears of joy as she regarded her daughter. In her heart she fervently hoped that tonight Temia would find romance.

She was concerned that Temia was almost twenty-two and showed no signs of being interested in marriage.

"You are so beautiful, Temia," she murmured.

The guests were now starting to arrive in increasing throngs and the carriages queued the length of the drive to discharge their glittering loads.

Lady Brandon was soon so engaged in greeting her guests that she temporarily forgot all her concerns.

In the ballroom Temia was quickly surrounded by young gentlemen, all eager to make her acquaintance.

"You have deprived the County of your beauty for too long," said one.

"You are a vision!" exclaimed another, leading her onto the dance floor.

"Say you will marry me or I will surely die of a broken heart!" professed another.

Having lived for so long in France, Temia simply laughed away these idle compliments and continued to change partners with each successive dance.

Halfway through the evening, she declared herself exhausted as she extricated herself from the arms of one, George Armstrong.

"You are breaking my heart, my angel!" he cried, clutching his chest in a theatrical gesture.

"I will return later," she smiled at him coquettishly, "now do dance with some other young lady."

Temia withdrew to the anteroom where there were comfortable sofas.

She smiled at the group of dowagers in the corner, who were fully occupied with the gossip of the evening – they were all chattering and whispering behind their fans as Temia sank down onto a chair.

As she relaxed, she was suddenly aware of a man by the door, whose eyes were burning into her.

For some reason she felt a distinct sense of unease.

She glanced over at him for the merest of seconds and he took that as his cue.

'Oh, no!' she said to herself, as she watched him march towards her.

"Hello, you are Miss Brandon, are you not?"

"I am, but you have me at a loss, sir. I am afraid we have not met before, have we?"

"Lord Alphonse at your service. No, we have not met, but I am a business acquaintance of your father."

"So, you are in the equine business?"

"In a manner of speaking, yes," he replied, a little obliquely. "He did not tell me he had such an enchantingly beautiful daughter – but you are not dancing?"

"I am a little tired. I have not left the dance floor since the music began."

"But you will dance with me, of course," he said, with the kind of overweening confidence that Temia found quite distasteful.

She looked up at Lord Alphonse and took in his tall figure and long face – and large nose that seemed to droop downwards. His hair was black but thinning and Temia judged him to be at least forty.

All in all, there was something about him that made her feel uncomfortable.

"I would like to rest awhile," she answered quietly.

"Nonsense! A lovely young lady like you? Come, the orchestra is playing a waltz. Grant me this one dance."

Temia thought that her father might be annoyed if she upset him, so she rose and took his proffered arm.

During the waltz, Lord Alphonse pressed himself just a little bit too close to her and Temia found the whole experience rather distasteful.

She could feel his growing attraction to her and, when she tried to pull herself away from his firm embrace, he moved even closer to her.

As the music stopped, he remained holding her.

"You dance divinely, Temia, and indeed you are very beautiful. Might I call on you tomorrow?"

"I am afraid I shall be occupied, Lord Alphonse. I have only just returned from France and am rather busy."

"I shall be visiting your father tomorrow morning, so, if you are here at home, I will see you," he persisted, releasing her. "Now, please excuse me – my carriage is waiting."

Temia felt her skin crawling as he kissed her hand.

Almost as soon as Lord Alphonse had left her side, her mother hurried over to her.

"What did he say? What did he talk about?" she asked in an anxious tone that made Temia suspect that this Lord Alphonse was a far more important person than she had at first suspected.

"He was most insistent that I allow him to call on me tomorrow. Of course, I shall say I am not at home."

"That is not wise, Temia, dear. He is a very good client of your father."

"But Mama, I don't care for him at all. He held me disagreeably close during the waltz and it – upset me."

"Darling, I feel certain that, if you can handle the attentions of Parisian men, then you are more than able to deal with him in the correct manner. You must not be too off-putting to him, darling, your father would not be happy if he took umbrage with us."

Temia felt a lump spring into her throat. She had not expected her Mama to say this.

Why was she not agreeing with her?

No gentleman would hold a lady he had just met so close!

'I can see that they wish to impress him and that I must go along with it,' she mused, as George Armstrong happened on her in the corridor.

But even as she danced with him, she could not wipe the vision of Lord Alphonse's leering face from her mind for the rest of the evening –

*

The servants were still clearing up after the ball when Temia went downstairs to find something to eat the following morning. It was almost midday, but she could not wait until luncheon.

Slipping down the backstairs and into the kitchen, she begged some bread and honey from Mrs. Duff who had just taken a batch of steaming loaves out of the oven.

She sat at the kitchen table and ate, famished.

'At least if I am down here, Ridley will not find me,' she said to herself.

But five minutes later he came down the stairs.

"Miss Temia! Now what are you doing here?"

"I wanted something to eat."

"A gentleman who is in with your father has been asking after you."

Temia sighed.

"Would that be a Lord Alphonse?" she asked.

"It is, miss."

"Ridley, I wish you to tell him, if he asks for me again, that I am not at home. Do you understand?"

"Very good, miss. And if the Master requests your presence?"

"You have not seen me."

The butler paused and then nodded, slowly. Taking up a salver he made his way back up the stairs.

After finishing her snack, she crept out of the back door and out into the grounds.

The Head Gardener was clearing leaves from the path and his assistant was busy pruning some bushes.

Without thinking, Temia soon found herself by the stables.

'I should not linger here,' she thought, 'for this is surely the one place Lord Alphonse will visit if he is here.'

As she turned back towards the house, she heard someone shout her name.

With a sinking heart, she ignored Lord Alphonse at first, but then, when his shouts became louder and more insistent, it would be rude not to acknowledge him.

Forcing a smile, she turned towards him.

He was hurrying across the courtyard towards her with his head bent.

"Miss Brandon! I was told you were not at home."

"Ridley could not find me, as I was in the kitchen. He must have assumed I was out."

"I am so glad I have seen you as there is an urgent matter I wish to discuss with you."

"I was just about to go out, Lord Alphonse."

"It will not take long. Can we go inside?"

"I must speak with Robert."

"Later. Come, let's return to the house. You must be cold without a coat or shawl."

He touched Temia's shoulder in a gesture that made her shudder. She did not like being treated so familiarly.

Once inside the house, she led him to the drawing room, hoping that her father would be there, but he was nowhere to be seen.

"Miss Brandon," he began. "You have to believe that I have thought of nothing but you since our meeting last night and I have to confess that I have fallen utterly in love with you. I am not a man to tarry when I have set my mind on something, and so, I ask you to marry me. I know that your father will agree to it."

"You have spoken of this to Papa?" asked Temia a little nervously.

"No, not yet, but I am most confident that he will not raise any objections to our betrothal."

Temia paused.

She did not wish to cause offence, but equally she was taken aback by the shocking arrogance of the man.

"I am afraid that I do not wish to marry anyone at present, Lord Alphonse," she replied stoutly. "Naturally I am flattered to be asked, but I am not able to accept. Now, if you will excuse me, as I have said, I am about to go out."

Lord Alphonse's face grew red with anger. His lip trembled and he exhaled noisily as he knitted his eyebrows.

"You – refuse – me?" he spluttered.

"I do," answered Temia quietly.

"What objection can you possibly have to refuse a gentleman of my standing?"

"Sir, I hardly know you. That is reason enough, is it not?"

"No, it is not!" he shouted. "I am used to getting what I want and I *will* have you, Miss Brandon! I will leave you for now to contemplate the error of your decision and will return tomorrow once you have had a chance to think about it. Good day. I will show myself out."

With that he stormed angrily out of the room.

She heard the front door slam shut and the sound of his footsteps dying away over the gravel.

'I fear I have made an enemy,' she said to herself, sitting down on the sofa. 'Papa will be furious, but surely, he will understand why I have refused?'

But in her heart, grew a nagging fear that perhaps, just as Lord Alphonse was not a man to be put off, her father was not going to be as understanding as she would hope.

CHAPTER THREE

While Temia was awake all that night, occupying her mind with unwanted thoughts about Lord Alphonse, in London the Earl of Wentworth was feeling agitated.

"What the hell do you mean, we cannot enter?" he demanded at the stage door with his silver-topped cane in his hand.

His tall frame was encased in a large black cloak and his silk hat made him seem even taller than his six feet.

"I'm sorry, my Lord, but Mr. Baker was insistent – no gentlemen callers backstage tonight."

"But my friend here is accompanying one of the young ladies to dinner," he asserted, tapping his long cane impatiently on the pavement. "Leo knows us!"

"Sorry, my Lord. I've got me orders."

The man shut the stage door abruptly, leaving him and Sir Thomas Babbington indignantly on the pavement.

"It's no problem, I can see Gladys another night," said Sir Thomas. "There was no need to make a fuss."

The Earl sighed.

It was not as if he was interested in any of the girls from *Les Jolies Mademoiselles*.

Since he had broken off an engagement two years earlier, he had steered clear of any romantic interludes. True, a man had needs, but these were easily satisfied by a stream of willing, usually married, ladies he encountered at endless balls and house parties.

But, of late, even those had ceased to amuse him.

His last *affaire du coeur* had ended when the lady in question had returned repentant to her husband.

On the other hand, Sir Thomas was an inveterate romancer of showgirls. It was one of his few vices that, unlike carousing or playing cards, the Earl did not share an enthusiasm for.

But Sir Thomas was a slave to a pretty ankle and a saucy wink and the actresses of London had provided him with many merry moments.

"I must break myself of this habit," he murmured as they returned to their carriage. "I should settle down with a nice girl from a good family and produce a son and heir. It is what my father would have wanted."

The Earl threw his head back and laughed.

"I would so like to meet the young lady who could tame you!" he cried. "No, I do believe that, in spite of your protestations, you are a dyed-in-the-wool bachelor! Shall we go instead to our Club, Thomas?"

"I suppose a brandy or two might help pass the time agreeably. Coachman! Take us to Whites."

The sleek black phaeton moved forward and soon they had left the lights of the *Royal Kent Theatre* behind.

*

Temia was right that Lord Alphonse was not a man to be easily deterred.

The day following her rejection of him, a large box of flowers appeared at Bovendon Hall.

"Orchids!" sighed her Mama. "They are lovely."

"Funeral flowers," countered Temia dismissively.

"But darling, these are not white. I have never seen such beautiful colours."

Temia read the card that came with the orchids.

"*I shall not rest until you say you will be mine.*"

The day was cold and the parlour maid had already lit the fire. Temia threw the card into the flames and then watched as it curled up and dissolved into cinders.

"Darling one, was that really necessary?"

Temia was still gazing at the flames.

"Shall I ask Sarah to put them in your room?"

"No, Mama. If they have to be displayed, let them stay in the hall, so I will not have to look at them for long."

Temia paced up and down by the window before, finally, hurling herself into an armchair.

"Temia!" cried her mother. "I don't think we paid all that money for you to go to Finishing School so you could throw yourself around like a stable boy! What if Ridley had been in the room?"

"Then he would have averted his eyes," answered Temia sulkily.

But even removing the orchids from the room did nothing to soothe her foul temper.

And when, that afternoon, a note arrived from Lord Alphonse saying he would be calling the next day, Temia was beside herself.

She ran out and took refuge in the stables, picking up a brush and grooming Lightning until his coat shone.

"Miss Temia, there be no need for you to do that, I was about to do it meself!" said Robert, as he came across her in Lightning's stall.

"It's no reflection on you," she replied, burying her face in Lightning's silky mane. "I wished to be out of the house."

"Shall I saddle him up for you, miss?"

Temia brightened visibly.

"What a wonderful idea! I shall ride to the village and back. A change of scenery is what I need."

The day was grey and overcast, but Temia did not pay any heed to the weather.

She rode Lightning hard and fast along the road to the village and stopped to look at her brother's memorial. The bronze relief of his likeness almost seemed to her like that of some other person and, as she stared at it, she could barely believe that Jasper was dead.

'How different my life might have been, had he lived,' she mused, touching the brass plaque affectionately before remounting Lightning.

*

At breakfast the following day, Temia was given strict instructions from her father that if Lord Alphonse should call, she must receive him.

"Papa, if he asks me to marry him again, I will not say 'yes'! Would you speak to him? Perhaps he would take my refusal more seriously if it came from you."

Sir Arthur looked distinctly uneasy.

Temia could see that he quite clearly did not wish to have any such conversation with Lord Alphonse.

"It may be difficult to broach the subject. There are outstanding matters I have to discuss with him first."

"But you will at least say my mind is made up?"

Sir Arthur hesitated and appeared uncomfortable with doing that favour for Temia. She was far too used to him allowing her to have her own way and his reluctance quite shocked her.

"You must not upset him, dearest. If you must refuse him once again, say that you have no wish to marry anyone – and do try not to offend him," added her Mama, anxiously.

"It's true, I don't wish to marry anyone. I have yet to meet a man who intrigues me enough for that. I want a man who is not showy and boastful – what would there be for me to discover about him otherwise?"

She then flounced out of the room.

Lady Brandon waited until she judged that Temia was out of earshot and turned to her husband,

"You *must* tell her, Arthur. If she knows the real reason for you wanting to keep him on your side, perhaps she will at least be a little more pleasant to him."

"Alice, I will not discuss my business or personal affairs with my daughter! Is it not enough that my wife knows I have made a damn fool of myself?"

"Then, you will only have yourself to blame if she inadvertently makes things worse."

*

But Temia's father did not speak with her and so Lord Alphonse came calling the next day, as he promised.

And Temia again refused his proposal of marriage.

Sir Arthur was now in the awful position of having to explain in detail to Lord Alphonse why his daughter had not accepted him.

He took the clearly annoyed Lord into his library and brought out his best brandy, hoping to soothe him.

"She is young, Lord Alphonse, and she has no wish to marry yet awhile," said Sir Arthur, handing him a glass.

"Your daughter is almost twenty-two and she will be an old maid if she persists in this foolishness. I intend to have her, Sir Arthur, and I would appreciate *your* help."

"Temia is very strong-willed and I cannot make her do anything she does not wish to."

Lord Alphonse looked at Sir Arthur with a distinct sneer on his face.

"I would not care to endure a tyrant in petticoats in my own home."

"Then, Temia would most certainly not prove to be a satisfactory wife for you, Lord Alphonse," answered Sir Arthur, hoping that would be an end to the matter.

"Ah," he countered, with a supercilious smile, "but I believe she is waiting to be tamed. I have yet to meet the woman I could not bend to my will, *if* I choose to do so."

He swigged at his brandy and laughed a low cruel laugh that made Sir Arthur feel quite ill.

"Now, to business," said Lord Alphonse, taking out his pocket book. "I believe you have some new stock that would interest me – "

Outside the library, Temia had stood listening to their raised voices through the door. Although she could not hear exactly, she could guess the drift.

'I hope that Papa has made it clear I don't welcome Lord Alphonse's wooing,' she murmured to herself.

She was still feeling a little ruffled from having to refuse him yet again. This time he had tried to control his temper and had simply laughed when she had said 'no'.

"A lady always refuses at first, otherwise she is not a lady," he had said in an infuriating manner. "You will agree eventually."

"*I will not!*" she had replied, her blue eyes flashing.

It was all she could do not to run out of the room and it was only the arrival of her father that had relieved the tension.

Temia then took the opportunity to excuse herself, ran upstairs and waited until they left the drawing room before making her way back down the stairs again.

And now she could hear raised voices no more and guessed that her father had opened his drinks cabinet where he kept his best brandy.

'I hope he has not gone against what he promised he would say,' she thought, suddenly panicking that the brandy meant a deal signed and sealed.

Just then, her Mama entered the hall and frowned.

"Listening at doorways? Really, Temia!"

"Mama, it's not what you might think. Papa is in there with Lord Alphonse. I have refused him yet again."

Lady Brandon sighed.

"He is a persistent man, I will grant you."

"Mama, if I could have dealt with him myself, I would not have involved Papa."

"Yes, I know, my dearest. Now come and let's go into the drawing room, as it would not do for the servants to catch us behaving like this."

"Servants?"

"Precisely. Do hurry now, it sounds as if they are finishing their discussions."

Temia and her mother quickly went to the drawing room and they were about to sit down when Lord Alphonse appeared at the door.

"Miss Brandon, Lady Brandon. I am sorry I cannot linger any longer, but I have business to deal with. I will see you again soon – in fact, *very soon*, indeed!"

He bowed and then took his hat from Ridley.

As Temia heard the front door close, she turned to her mother,

"What did he mean by that? Very soon indeed."

"I really don't know, dearest."

Ridley now reappeared in the drawing room and his face wore a grave look.

"My Lady, the Master asks for you in the library, if you could come at once."

Ridley had no liking for Lord Alphonse, but would never have made his feelings known. He did not care for the way the man looked around The Hall as if he was about to assume ownership of it.

"Temia, I must leave you. I trust you will be dining with us this evening?"

"Yes, Mama. I have no other engagements. I had quite forgotten how very quiet life can be in the country."

Lady Brandon's heart sank, as she sensed that her summons to the library was to do with Lord Alphonse.

It was fortunate that Temia was otherwise engaged when her mother finally emerged from the library over an hour later looking tearful and drawn.

She gave instructions to Ridley that she was not to be disturbed before dinner and then retired to her room.

She was dreading the evening because when Lord Alphonse had alluded to the fact that he would see them again very soon, it had not been an idle boast.

She did not know if she should warn Temia that he was coming to dinner this evening and that he would once more propose, but this time with her father's blessing.

Temia had retired to the music room and spent the hours before dinner amusing herself by playing the piano.

Her fingers flew across the keys in a lively Chopin piece and then Beethoven. She felt herself transported by the sadness of the *Moonlight Sonata* and even more so by his *Adagio cantabile* from his No. 8 in C minor.

Temia played fluidly with a refined elegance that had often been commented on when she was in Paris.

She loved music and enjoyed playing the very fine grand piano that had once been her grandmother's.

She played as if she had not a care in the world, little realising that her nice comfortable life was soon to change dramatically.

"Miss, please keep still or else I'll never get your hair right!"

Sarah was indignant that Temia appeared unable to stop moving her head while she was pulling her hair into an elaborate style.

At last she put the final pin in the back and Temia was ready.

"Very good, Sarah," exclaimed Temia, admiring her reflection.

It did not matter to her one jot that there was no one to impress with her fine looks apart from her parents – she had learned in Paris that one should always look one's best at all times and in all places.

The gong sounded and she was now quite hungry as she had not eaten much at luncheon.

The blue satin of her gown matched the colour of her eyes perfectly and the sapphire brooch on her bosom added a pleasing touch.

Her Mama was already in the dining room when she entered and was in conversation with Ridley.

"Ah, Temia, dearest. Papa is keeping us waiting, I am afraid."

"Where is he?"

"In the drawing room entertaining our guest."

Temia looked startled.

"I did not realise that we were expecting one," she murmured, taking a seat.

She was about to enquire as to who it might be, when her father came in to the room – with Lord Alphonse close behind him.

"Miss Brandon, may I say how delightful you look this evening?" he began, as his eyes raked up and down her frame like a hungry wolf eyeing its prey.

"Lord Alphonse," she replied, stiffening a little.

She stared at her father, who did not meet her eye.

'So, this was Papa's doing,' she thought, feeling utterly betrayed as, far from discouraging Lord Alphonse's attentions, he now sought to endorse them by inviting him to dine with them!

'How could he?' she fumed, feeling a lump rising in her throat.

She was so upset it quite ruined her appetite.

Lord Alphonse sat next to her, staring at her all the way through dinner.

"You are not eating, Miss Brandon," he remarked, as yet another full plate of food was taken away.

"I am feeling rather unwell," she replied, as politely as she could. "Papa, might I retire?"

"I would prefer that you remain at the table until the meal is over, Temia," he answered her sternly.

She had a terrible idea that after dinner she would have to endure another proposal from Lord Alphonse.

'Why does Papa not pay attention to my wishes? He has never before attempted to push me into finding a husband and I have only just returned home – so why is he doing this?'

She managed to eat most of her apple tart and made her coffee last for as long as possible.

Finally, her parents looking at each other in a knowing fashion, rose from their chairs and excused themselves.

"Temia," said her father a little awkwardly. "We shall leave you two alone for a while and take our coffee into the drawing room."

Before Temia could open her mouth to protest, they had both withdrawn and closed the door behind them.

She then heard Lord Alphonse cough to gain her attention and reluctantly, she turned to face him.

"Temia – I may call you that, may I not? I have asked you twice now to marry me and both times you have refused me. But this time, when I ask you, I want you to carefully consider your response."

Taking a small box out of his pocket, he opened it to reveal a magnificent sapphire and diamond engagement ring.

Temia could not help but let out a gasp.

It was lovely and a superb piece of craftsmanship. She knew at once that it must have cost a fortune and yet nothing would persuade her to sell herself for just a trinket.

Lord Alphonse then went down on one knee before her and took her left hand in his.

"Temia, I ask you once more, will you marry me?"

She could not take her eyes off the glittering ring he held in his fingers. Its beauty was so amazing and, from another man, she would have wept with joy to receive it.

She took a deep breath and shook her head firmly,

"I am sorry, Lord Alphonse, but I have no wish to – marry."

As her last words died away, Lord Alphonse's face changed. A cruel gleam came into his eyes and he refused to let go of her hand, grasping her even more tightly.

"You are hurting me," she cried trying to stay calm.

"And is that your final word?"

"I shall not change my mind," she answered him, looking down at the floor.

In a gesture that took her breath away for its sheer brutality, Lord Alphonse rammed the ring onto her third finger and held it fast.

Tears sprang into her eyes.

"My dear," he said in a voice like ice, "you have no choice in the matter. This afternoon your father agreed to our engagement and early wedding. It is all settled and you shall be my wife before the month is out."

"No!" screamed Temia, wrenching her hand away and standing up. "Never! Papa would never agree to it."

As she ran out of the room, she heard him laugh.

"Go, run to your Papa! He will tell you the same thing – that today he promised you to me."

Temia then burst into the drawing room to find her Mama in tears by the fire and her Papa standing with his back to her by the window.

There was a strained atmosphere in the room and she was shocked that her father was ignoring her Mama in such a cold manner.

"Papa? Is it true what Lord Alphonse says?" she screamed, trying to pull the tight ring off her finger.

"*It is.*"

"But how could you? You know I have no wish to marry him and yet you agreed? *Why*? Why?"

Lady Brandon looked up and dabbed her eyes.

"You must tell her now, Arthur. She deserves an explanation."

Temia stared wildly at her father.

She suddenly no longer recognised the once benign man she called her Papa since she could talk. This stranger who stood before her, so cold and unfeeling – he was not her father!

"Tell me what, Mama?"

Lady Brandon sobbed and Temia had never seen her mother display such naked emotion since the day they had received word of her brother's death.

"Temia." Her Papa cleared his throat awkwardly. "The reason I have agreed to this marriage is that Lord Alphonse has made it clear that unless it proceeds, he will reveal a rather unsavoury episode from my past."

"He is attempting to blackmail you? Papa, whatever it is, can we not rise above it?"

Her father shook his head dejectedly.

"No. We cannot. You *will* marry Lord Alphonse."

Temia drew herself up to her full height.

How could she make her feelings known without appearing disrespectful to her father?

"So, you have agreed to hand me over like a mare to a stud?" she whispered, daring him to meet her gaze. "What is it, this secret that is so terrible that you would sacrifice the happiness of your only surviving child?"

Lady Brandon's sobs rent the air.

"Arthur, *tell her*!" she exhorted.

"Georgiana alluded to something when I saw her in London," asserted Temia bravely. "I think I am now old enough to know the truth, however distasteful it might be. Perhaps then, I can begin to understand."

Sir Arthur's own eyes were clouded with tears, as he stared into the middle distance. His jaw worked and his mouth was thin and tight.

"Before I married your Mama – I was young and foolish. I was involved with a dancer and a child was born. Lord Alphonse discovered this secret and is threatening to ruin my reputation with it. He has been blackmailing me for months and taking horses from me without payment.

"If he cannot have you, then he will ensure that we will have no place in polite Society and we shall have to sell up everything and move to Scotland or Ireland, where people will not know us.

"Temia – I am too old to start my life – *anew*!"

His voice nearly broke on the last word and, almost collapsing, he sat down in a chair near the fire and took his wife's hand.

Temia stared at her parents in horror.

To think that the great family secret was this!

"And the child? Did he or she live?"

"I believe so, but the mother was paid off and I never saw her again."

"So," stammered Temia, the gravity of her situation sinking home. "I have a half-brother or sister out there? Would you have told me had this situation not arisen?"

Sir Arthur shook his head.

"Probably not, dearest. I don't even know if she grew to adulthood."

"She? I have a half-sister! And the mother?"

"We just don't know where she is or if she is still alive," interrupted Lady Brandon. "Temia, the only way to keep this dreadful matter secret is for you to marry him."

"But I cannot!" she protested.

"For the love of God, Temia. If you honour me and love me as you should, *you will*!"

The tone in his voice was little short of desperate, but there was no mistaking his absolute determination.

Unable to contain herself any longer, Temia fled from the room and ran upstairs. Locking her bedroom door, she threw herself on the bed and sobbed into the pillows.

Her finger throbbed from the effort of trying to take off the dreaded ring, but the more she had pulled, the more her finger swelled, making it impossible to budge it.

'I must be calm and I must think,' she told herself, drying her tears on a handkerchief.

'I would rather die than marry that man. It would not be such a bad thing if we moved away to Scotland – I would not care! At least we could be together as a family.'

But she knew that her Mama would not cope so far away from her friends and had her Papa not said that he could not face the prospect?

'If I am to avoid marriage to that odious man, then there is only one course of action,' she determined.

The two years she had spent in France had made her a very independent young woman and she did not fear being on her own and indeed positively thrived on it.

'*I* am not too young to start anew,' she sighed to herself, coming to a decision. 'And, so, if I remove myself from the equation, then surely Lord Alphonse will leave Papa alone? I could become a Governess and make my own way in the world. I could teach French and music – '

The more she thought about it, the more viable it appeared to her.

'I could stay in London with Georgiana and swear her to secrecy until I find a post. It should not be difficult. Perhaps I shall go abroad and as far away from that hateful man as possible.

'Yes,' she concluded at last. 'If I simply disappear, then Lord Alphonse cannot force Papa's hand. It would be best for everyone if I run away!'

With her mind made up, Temia then began to plot her escape from Bovendon Hall.

That very night!

CHAPTER FOUR

Now that her mind was made up, Temia did not hesitate.

She then packed herself a small suitcase, taking just enough clothes with her to last a week or so.

After applying a great deal of soap, she managed to prise the hated ring from her finger and left it, together with a note to her parents, with a PS that read,

"Please return this ring to Lord Alphonse."

With everything now in place, she then undressed and climbed into bed.

She found it hard to sleep, but managed to snatch a few hours, waking in the hour before dawn.

Temia guessed that none of the servants would be up, but she hoped that Robert would be stirring, as without his help she could not carry out her plan.

She crept downstairs and let herself out through the French windows.

The sun was just about beginning to rise.

She knew that the first train out of Northampton Station left quite early. And she intended to be on it!

She could see that an oil lamp was burning in one of the stalls as she approached the stable block.

'I do hope that's Robert and not one of the stable boys,' she murmured, as she hurried towards the light.

"Now, what in God's name be you doin' up at this hour, miss?"

She heaved a sigh of relief, as Robert came towards her with a bucket of water in one hand.

"Robert, I need your help," she began simply.

"Well, if I can be of any service – " he answered in a way that was more of a question than an answer.

"I need to go to Northampton Station at once!"

"At once? What's the 'urry, miss?"

"I wish to catch the first train."

"Does the Master know about this?"

Temia looked down at the hay on the floor.

"I have an early appointment in London. Now, will you take me or must I drive myself and let the brougham come back on its own?"

Robert clucked his tongue as if weighing it up.

"Very good, miss."

"And there is a suitcase to fetch from my room."

As Robert made his way across the courtyard to the main house, she congratulated herself for giving a plausible reason so fast and she was counting on her lack of luggage not arousing his suspicions.

The minutes ticked by agonisingly.

The sun was by now casting thin beams across the courtyard and she could hear the horses beginning to stir in their stalls. One of the stable boys ran across the yard and, seeing her, doffed his cap.

Temia froze and wished that Robert would hurry.

So she was flooded with relief when he came into sight with the case in his hand.

Robert ordered the stable boy to hitch up the small buggy and put her case into the rear compartment.

"You'll have to sit on the box with me, miss."

"That will be quite all right, Robert," she answered, wrapping her cloak around her, "but can we leave at once? The Station is some miles off and the train leaves at six."

Robert grunted, helped Temia up onto the box and then climbed up next to her.

As they drove off, Temia did not look behind her. She knew that if she did, she would surely cry.

She was relieved when, just over an hour later, they finally drew up outside the Station.

She thanked Robert profusely and then, with a tear in her eye, waved him goodbye.

As she bought her ticket, her heart beat so wildly it took her breath away.

'London!' she muttered to herself. '*A new life*!'

*

Temia always felt a thrill of excitement whenever she visited London and today was no exception.

The Hackney cab she hired at Euston Station made its way through the crowded streets and, once again, she was struck by the smells and sounds of the Capital.

'Even though London is dirty and noisy, it's still a really wonderful place to be!' she thought, as the cab made laborious progress through the traffic.

At last they arrived at Campden Hill Road.

'I do hope that Aunt Marianne and Georgiana are at home,' she said to herself, as she rang the doorbell. 'It's strange that Bob's not barking.'

After what felt like an age, the door opened and there stood, not the butler, but an unfamiliar maid.

"Is my aunt at home?" she asked nervously.

"I'm afraid not, Miss – "

"Brandon. And my cousin, Georgiana?"

"Both gone away, Miss Brandon. They left on a whim last night. Gone to Brighton for the sea air."

Temia stood still, her mind whirling. She had not anticipated this.

"I don't know when they'll be back. They could be gone a few days or a few weeks, they didn't say."

"Thank you," said Temia faintly.

She turned back to the cab, thankful she had not sent it away as how else could she have managed her case?

"If you needs lodgings, my sister runs a genteel boarding house for young ladies of your class," suggested the driver. "It be on the other side of the High Street."

"Yes, thank you. I would be most grateful," replied Temia, almost not thinking what she was doing.

The lodgings house was as the driver had described it – clean, neat and comfortable. She paid the woman in advance for one night and then went straight out again.

As she walked to the crossroads, she saw the *Royal Kent Theatre*. How different it seemed in the daytime!

Wandering round to the side, she noticed that a set of the theatre's double doors was open.

'How intriguing!' she muttered to herself, suddenly feeling the spirit of adventure rise in her again.

She quickly looked to see if anyone was about and then she slipped inside the door.

Almost at once, she found herself in a pale-cream corridor that smelled musty and strange and she followed it along to another set of doors.

From a distance she could hear the sound of a lone piano playing and a man's voice barking out orders.

'*Rehearsals*,' she thought excitedly, slowly pushing open the heavy mahogany door.

She had never seen the inside of a theatre during the daytime before and her first impression was how faded the drapes and trimmings on the boxes appeared.

On the stage half a dozen girls were going through their paces, wearing scandalously short dresses that only just covered their knees. Underneath they wore thick black stockings and flat slippers.

"One-two-three, *step*!" shouted the man from the front of the stalls.

He was in his mid-forties and sported long whiskers that stuck out either side of his ruddy face. He appeared to be the Director and was remonstrating with the dancers that they were not working hard enough.

"I want this new *Woodland Nymph Dance* included this weekend – not next year!" he bellowed. "Now, try it again and put your backs into it!"

The piano struck up again and the dancers whirled and twirled, kicking their legs in unison.

Temia thought the dance was lively enough, but the scenery behind them was dull and unattractive.

'I used to paint much better work than that in my art class in Paris,' she reflected. 'And my woodland scene for the end-of-term concert was far superior to theirs.'

After a while, the Director called a halt to the dance and disappeared off backstage.

The girls began to chatter and rub their tired limbs, while one peeled an apple and ate it noisily.

'So these are *Les Jolies Mademoiselles*!' thought Temia, scrutinising the girls' faces. They all seemed quite young and, apart from one or two who clearly wore make-up, well-scrubbed.

Just then, a man came onstage and announced that they were taking a break.

The girls filed off noisily, leaving Temia alone in the auditorium.

As she sat there, an idea occurred to her. Rather than be a Governess, might she not offer her services as a scenery painter?

With her heart in her mouth, she strode towards the stage and called up to the man from the stalls.

"Excuse me, could you tell me who is in charge of this troupe? I would like to speak with him."

"It's Mr. Leo Baker, you'll be wantin'," he said, picking up a broom and sweeping the stage. "If you 'urry, you'll catch 'im through them doors on your right."

Not wishing to waste time, Temia hurried to the front and through the doors the man had indicated, where she found herself in another corridor at the end of which was an Office.

She could hear Leo Baker's booming voice through the frosted-glass door, so she knocked and waited.

After a pause came a voice,

Enter!"

Temia gingerly opened the door and stepped inside.

Leo Baker was talking with a young boy, who was balancing a pile of costumes in his arms.

"Yes?" he asked. "Can I help you, madam?"

"My name is Miss Morris," she began, changing her name. "I – I wish to speak to you about your scenery."

"What about it? I know it's not much, but with my overheads, we can't afford new so we make do with what we've got!"

"I was going to offer you my services as an artist."

"You? I didn't think ladies did such things."

"I have experience in painting scenery and if you don't believe me, let me make a new backdrop for that dance you were rehearsing – the *Woodland Nymph*."

Leo Baker continued to regard her closely.

"It's true we've had the same scenery for twenty years and this piece is meant to be the finale for our new show. I cannot deny that brand new scenery would greatly enhance the effect and bring in the customers."

"Let me try, please. All I would ask is for food and lodgings."

"So you'd do it for nothing? And all I have to do is put you up with the girls?"

"Yes, although, if there were some other paid work available, I would be happy to consider it. I am able to sew and am a hard worker."

Leo Baker was a man very much disposed towards a bargain and here was one if ever he saw it.

'Another runaway,' he said to himself, 'but this one appears to come from a good home.'

"You're not in *trouble*, are you?" he asked warily.

"Trouble?"

He hesitated at Temia's display of innocence. He would have to think carefully how to explain this to her, as she was obviously a lady of some delicacy.

"You have not had your virtue compromised and have run away from your family?"

Temia suddenly understood what he was alluding to and laughed out loud.

"Goodness, no! I intended to stay with a cousin and arrived without warning to find she had gone away."

"Very well," Leo Baker said suddenly. "If I have Hobson bring you out an old screen, could you paint it for me? It will be a test."

"Of course."

"Then, come with me. Have it done by five o'clock and I will make my decision then."

He then rose from his desk and led Temia up some stairs. Within seconds they were in a labyrinth of corridors that appeared to wind their way around the building.

"Goodness! I would be lost if you were not leading the way," she commented, as they reached the stage.

"Hobson! Hobson!"

Leo Baker shouted into the auditorium and soon the man Temia had spoken to earlier appeared beneath them.

"Yes, Mr. Baker."

"Go and get that old screen from the dressing room and some paint from the store. This young lady, Miss – ?"

"Morris."

"Yes, she's going to paint it for us."

Hobson simply nodded and disappeared again.

"Just wait here for him and put your things by the piano, if you like. Keep out of the way of the girls when they come back – there's plenty of room, but mind you don't splash paint all over the place."

Temia undid her bonnet and took off her gloves.

She hoped that she would be able to work in such a cold place and it would not affect her ability.

To her surprise, after bringing her the screen and paint, Hobson also brought her a cup of tea.

Temia threw herself into painting the screen.

She turned it into a woodland glade with birds and trees, working as hard as she could. Her fingers almost froze as she worked, but Hobson brought her another cup of tea that warmed her all through.

The girls returned after their break and immediately came to see what she was doing.

"Coo, look at that!" came a Cockney accent.

"Blimey, ain't it just like bein' in Eppin' Forest?" answered her friend, a thin girl with curly red hair.

"Well, I think that it's very nice," said another girl, more quietly. She had dark hair and blue eyes that danced in a heart-shaped face. Temia liked her immediately.

"What you doin' this for?"

"I have asked Mr. Baker to employ me. I am doing this to show him my abilities."

"Like, when we audition?" giggled one of them.

"Yes."

"Come along, girls. Miss Morris is busy and you should be warming up!"

Leo Baker's strident tones rang across the stage and made the girls jump. The dark-haired girl smiled at Temia.

"Good luck!" she said, before joining the others.

By four o'clock, Temia had done as much as she could. She had almost run out of paint, so she put down her brushes and sighed.

Les Jolies Mademoiselles had rehearsed two dances and now, the red-haired girl, whose name was Lily, she discovered, was on stage alone.

Her singing voice had a pleasant tone, and, as she wrung her hands and cast her eyes skywards, she sang Handel's *Where'er you walk* to the piano.

As the last notes died away, Leo Baker came on to the stage and clapped his hands.

"Very good, Lily, that will have them dabbing their eyes! Now, let's see what Miss Morris has done."

He walked over to Temia.

"Well, there's a pretty thing," he called, taking in the woodland scene she had so vividly recreated. "Very good, very good indeed, Miss Morris, I would be delighted to employ you on the terms we discussed, of course."

"Of course," reiterated Temia. "And paid work?"

Leo Baker's face creased into a frown. He realised that Temia would be an asset and the girls were always complaining about doing their own hair and make-up?

"Do you think that you could paint faces as well as scenery? I could offer you a modest sum if you could and it would be modest, mind you."

Temia had already calculated that the amount she had in her bank account would last her six months and that would include paying for lodgings and food.

And now she was being offered both of these and a small sum.

"I would suppose that painting a face is no different to painting a canvas, so yes, thank you, I would like to take up your kind offer," she smiled.

Leo Baker stared at her for a long moment.

"You that sure you aren't interested in performing? With a face like yours, you'd pack 'em in! There's nothing these well-to-do gents like better than a pretty face and a nice ankle – they don't care so much about the voice!"

"No, thank you," said Temia blushing.

"Oh, never mind," he replied cheerfully. "Sophia, Look after this young lady, will you? She can stay in your room – there's a spare bed there since Gladys left us?"

To Temia's delight, it was the pleasant-looking girl with the dark hair who stepped forward.

"What's your name?" she asked.

"Temia."

"Well, Temia, our lodgings are not far from here. The landlady, Mrs. Hook, is quite stern, but she keeps a clean house."

"Oh, but I have already paid for a night in a nearby establishment."

"Then, we'll go there together and ask her to rent the room. You might lose your money, mind."

Sophia took her to the dressing room and Temia was entranced by the row of mirrors and the long narrow bench that served as a dressing table for the girls.

"You mean – you *all* use this room?" she asked.

"Where else?" said Sophia, "you'll get used to it. But it's not for the shy – when we're all in our underthings – oh, what those toffs would do to be in here!"

"Toffs?"

"You know, upper-class gents. You get all kinds of fellas who like to be around us – rich, not-so rich, bankers, types and even Lords! The girl whose bed you'll be having, Gladys, had a proper swell take a fancy to her. Thomas, his name was – can't remember who he was Lord of, but he was a Lord all right!"

Temia nodded in response. She had heard of such things. Aristocratic gentlemen who liked to consort with theatrical types. Had not King Charles II himself chosen a mistress from the Halls of Covent Garden?

"I – hope I haven't shocked you," added Sophia.

"Not at all. I lived in Paris for two years and the French are far more adventurous than the English."

"You'll get used to those gentlemen. We have ones come in here who think just because we're on stage, we've no morals – if you understand my meaning. Now, come and we'll go to your lodgings, Temia."

Her heart beat wildly as Sophia took her arm and led her onto the street.

As they walked away from the theatre, Temia could not resist one backward glance, just to convince herself that she was not dreaming.

'I am really part of *Les Jolies Mademoiselles*! What would Papa say?'

*

The lodgings where *Les Jolies Mademoiselles* were staying was neat and clean, even if Mrs. Hook was rather forbidding.

"No gentlemen callers," she said sternly, as Temia and Sophia struggled up the stairs with her suitcase.

The room was spacious enough for the two of them and comprised two beds and a washstand and Temia felt that it would be comfortable enough.

With a pain in her heart, she suddenly thought of home and her Mama and Papa.

"I must write a letter," she muttered.

"I have a sheet of paper," offered Sophia, hunting around in the small cupboard that stood at the end of the two beds. "But you will have to write it in your lap."

Temia found a wooden tray and began to write,

"*Dear Mama and Papa,*

I am sorry to have left you so suddenly. I write now to tell you that I am safe and well. Please don't try to find me. I will write again soon.

Your loving daughter, Temia."

"I wish I had someone to write to," sighed Sophia, wistfully watching Temia fold up her letter and address it. "But, it's no use wasting time wishing. Don't take off your bonnet, Temia, we have to return to the theatre soon. We have a show to do!"

It was dusk by the time they returned to the theatre. The lights were on and it was magically transformed into the wonderland she had glimpsed a few weeks earlier.

Sophia took her straight to the dressing room and showed her where the make-up box was kept.

"I hope you're quick. You've twelve girls to make up and help dress."

"Will I be able to see the show?" asked Temia, as she began to paint Lily's face.

"You can watch from the wings, but don't get in the way or Leo Baker will shout at you!"

Lily laughed.

"Cor, ain't you made me look a real lady?"

She admired her reflection and Temia could see her visibly preening.

"Won't that have the gents all clamourin' for me after the show!"

"You've told 'er about all them men, haven't you?" asked Lily, cocking her thumb at Temia.

"Yes, Lily. She knows!" answered Sophia.

"His Nibs is goin' to be mighty disappointed if 'e shows up tonight and finds Gladys gone. Perhaps he'll buy *me* supper instead!"

Temia's curiosity was now aroused. Who was this mysterious gentleman they spoke of?

"I'd rather dine with that there friend of his," said Blanche, "them flashin' eyes!"

"He be dangerous that one," came in another. "Got a right temper on him. Jim said he cut up somethin' rotten when he didn't let them in the other night."

Temia concentrated on the girls' faces and then, as they ran off for their first piece, she went to the wings.

Never had she encountered such a feeling!

She could almost touch the audience and feel their excitement and, when it came to the finale, she felt as if the applause would lift her up to the top of the theatre.

After the show she helped the girls hang up their costumes. It seemed as if she had barely finished before there came a knock on the dressing room door.

"Are you decent?"

"As we'll ever be, Jim!" called out Lily saucily.

The stage door manager put his head around the door and said,

"Two toffs be outside askin' for Gladys and won't believe she's not 'ere and want to see for themselves."

"So, let them in!" cried Lily, patting her hair and wetting her lips.

Next there came another knock at the door.

Temia busied herself with a pile of dresses and tried not to stare as the two gentlemen came into the room.

"Ladies – !" one of them began.

He was tall and handsome with mischievous blue eyes, golden-brown hair and a clipped moustache.

"Where on earth is Gladys? That bounder on the door said she was no longer here."

"She's not, milord," said Lily, sashaying towards him with a cute smile. "But I am and I don't have a dining companion this evening."

Temia stole a glance towards the two men and was at once drawn to the dark-haired man behind his friend.

He was about an inch taller and his face wore an impenetrable brooding look. His black hair curled over his ears and his eyes were flashing and yet mysterious.

Catching Temia's glance, he returned it with a look of such intensity that it hit Temia like a bolt of lightning.

As if by instinct, the first man followed his friend's stare and smiled delightedly at Temia.

"And who is this? You are new, are you not?"

"That's our new wardrobe mistress, scenery painter and general skivvy!" pouted Lily boldly.

Sir Thomas ignored her and walked up to Temia and, taking her hand, kissed it.

"Please forgive me," he said, "I am so overcome by your beauty I cannot resist! You must let me make amends for my impertinence by inviting you to dine with me – with us. I am Sir Thomas Babbington and this is my friend, the Earl of Wentworth."

'Wentworth!' thought Temia, in shock. 'Is this the very same Wentworth who had sent his apologies for not attending my ball?'

She was still rooted to the spot when Sir Thomas repeated his request.

Over his shoulder Temia could see Lily was red with fury. She stormed out of the dressing room, slamming the door behind her.

"I really – cannot!" stammered Temia blushing red.

"You wound me, madam, but no matter, as I shall return tomorrow evening and will endeavour to secure your acceptance then."

With a flourish he bowed low and turned to leave.

Behind him, the Earl of Wentworth was still staring at Temia and it caused her stomach to turn over.

"Good evening, ladies," he intoned in a deep rich voice that surprised her.

"Well then, you made a friend and an enemy!" said Sophia. "Lily didn't look so happy with you – unlike Sir Thomas there."

Temia did not speak again until they returned to their room at Mrs. Hook's.

She could not utter a word. How could she when her mind was spinning and her heart felt so strange? It was as if it had been pierced and looked into at the same time.

As they got ready for bed, she noticed that Sophia took out an old scrap of paper and kissed it.

Sophia caught Temia's look and tucked it away.

"It's a letter from the man who is my father," she said almost apologetically. "You'll think it rather foolish of me kissing it like that, but it's all I have of him."

"Do you know if your father is still alive?"

"I have no idea. I don't even know who he was."

She paused and then, as if weighing up whether or not to divulge something, took a deep breath.

"You'll not think ill of me if I tell you the truth?"

"No," answered Temia, taking her hand.

"Those two gentlemen who came in tonight – "

"My own father was one such gentleman – and my mother, she gave birth to me as a result. He was not a bad man, he gave Mama money, but I never met him. Mama would not tell me who he was. She took that secret to her grave. And all I do know is that he owned a big house in Northamptonshire, somewhere."

Temia's blood began to run cold.

"And you say you never saw him? Sophia, how old are you?"

"What a question to ask! A lady should never tell her age, that is for certain."

"How old are you?" repeated Temia. "Sophia, this is important. I want you to tell me the truth."

"Twenty-five," she whispered. "I'll be twenty-six in December."

The room swam in front of Temia's eyes.

She did not know what to think.

Twenty-six? That would be just one year older than Jasper would have been, had he lived.

"Sophia," she said, trying to keep her voice steady. "The letter – did he not sign it? Was there not a name?

"Only an initial. Would you like to see it?"

Temia hesitated.

If indeed her suspicions were correct, then she did not know how she would cope.

Swallowing hard, Temia nodded.

'I *must* see it! I must!' she told herself. 'If only to disperse these wicked thoughts in my mind!'

Sophia pulled the letter out of its hiding place and handed it to Temia. The paper was creased and faded.

With shaking hands she unfolded the letter and did not dare to examine the contents.

"*My dear Maria*," it began.

Temia did not need to read any further, for she only too clearly recognised the elegant handwriting.

But what would she say to Sophia?

The girl sat opposite her with her large eyes looking up at Temia, waiting for some kind word and yet, what she was about to tell her could change her life for ever.

How would she receive the news?

Taking a deep breath, at last, Temia spoke.

Her voice trembled as she carefully folded the note.

"Sophia," she said, "you may not believe me, but I have reason to believe that you and I are half-sisters!"

CHAPTER FIVE

"Sisters? How can that be?" cried Sophia, throwing her hands to her face. "I've dreamed of something like this happening, but now it has, I just don't believe it!"

"This," replied Temia, indicating the letter, "is my father's hand. Furthermore, I must tell you that there have been rumours of a dalliance that resulted in a child. This was before I was born or Papa met Mama, of course. And now, seeing this letter, the mystery is solved."

Sophia stared at Temia as if searching her face for clues to their shared parentage.

"I can scarcely believe it!" she repeated in shock. "*You* – my half-sister!"

"Did your mother never talk about your father?"

"Not a great deal. After he had paid for my birth, she cut off all contact with him. They were not in love and Mama said she knew he would never consider marrying her, as they were not of the same class. And by the time I was born, he had met your Mama."

"Sophia, I feel so terrible! All those years – "

"Temia," she interrupted, "you won't tell anyone how old I really am, will you? It's just that Leo Baker likes us young and fresh. I've told him I'm twenty-two!"

"Your secret is safe, Sophia. After all, you are now nursing an even bigger one that involves me!"

The two girls sat in silence for a while and Temia noticed that Sophia was crying.

"What is it, Sophia?"

"To think – all these years and I had a half-sister!"

"*And* a half-brother! Sadly he is no longer with us. He was killed in the Crimea five years ago."

"Oh! Dead before I knew him!"

"He was no more than a boy when he was killed, barely nineteen years old."

"Terrible! Terrible! And your – our Papa?"

"He is alive and well. We own a large house in Northamptonshire and he breeds horses. It was a hobby that became more than that."

"I dreamed my Papa was rich and handsome! Tell me more of him," pleaded Sophia. "Is he tall? Does he ride in a magnificent carriage?"

Temia laughed and then chose her words carefully.

"He is all those and more. But circumstances don't favour a meeting between you at present."

"Oh, I would not ask for such a thing! It's more than enough for me that I have met *you*! My sister!"

"Half-sister. Your Mama – what did she die of?"

"TB," answered Sophia, "it was awful how quickly it took her. I was lucky I didn't catch it too. It must be my blue blood! I miss Mama dreadfully."

"I understand. I miss Jasper. If I could speak with him or hear his voice one last time, I would not feel he was snatched away so suddenly."

"Oh, but there is a way," replied Sophia quietly.

Temia stared at her.

"How can there be? You can't speak to the dead!"

"It is not as impossible as you think, Temia. If you have faith. I receive messages from Mama all the time or rather I go to a lady who does."

"A lady who speaks to the dead?"

"Yes, she is a Mrs. Sebright and she's a brilliant spiritualist. She has the power to contact the dead and passes on their messages."

"But, this all sounds too incredible – if I thought I could speak to Jasper again, I would pay a lot for it!"

"Oh, Mrs. Sebright is very reasonable. She holds a circle once a month in Marylebone. Her next one's in a few weeks' time, why don't you come with me, Temia?"

Temia stared at Sophia. She did not know what to think. It was all so incredible.

"Come, Sophia, it's late. We must sleep – we shall talk more of this tomorrow."

As she put her head on the pillow, Temia could not believe how eventful her day had been.

'And now, this! A woman who claims to speak to the dead!' she mused, as she slowly drifted off to sleep.

*

As soon as Temia arrived at the theatre the next day, Leo Baker took her to a massive new canvas.

"Do you think you can manage to do this in time for our opening at *The Olympic Theatre*?" he said, showing her a row of paint tins. "Hobson will bring you ladders and I can employ a boy to help you, if you need it."

"When do you open at *The Olympic*?"

"In two weeks time."

"If I work very hard and have some help, it will be ready," answered Temia, rolling up her sleeves.

Taking her piece of charcoal and some paper that she had sectioned off into squares, she began to roughly sketch out a plan of the new scenery.

She became so engrossed in what she was doing that she did not hear the doors to the auditorium open and so, when Sir Thomas Babbington called to her from the stalls, she jumped out of her skin.

"Oh, I am very sorry!" he said. "I did not wish to surprise you in that manner. Please accept my apologies."

"Sir Thomas. What entices you here?"

"If I have come at an inopportune time, then I shall leave at once," he replied, putting on his top hat.

"No – I can work while we talk."

"Excellent! I shall join you on stage then, as I have no wish to shout at you."

As he appeared on the stage, a warm smile on his face, she found herself wishing that the Earl of Wentworth was with him.

"What brings you to the theatre, Sir Thomas, before a performance?" asked Temia. "It seems a pity to destroy one's illusions by seeing it in daylight."

"Can you not guess?" he asked with his blue eyes twinkling. "I came here because of you! I did not sleep a wink last night thinking of you and I wished to find out for myself if you are as beautiful at daytime as at night.

"And what do I find? You are a woman of many faces. You are fascinating, Temia – utterly enchanting!"

Temia blushed and tried hard to concentrate on her plan for the scenery.

"In addition I wonder what brought you here. You are not the type to be a showgirl. I know a lady when I see one and you, my dear, are a lady!"

"You flatter me," replied Temia, turning to face the blank canvas in front of her. "I am nothing special."

He moved towards her and stared into her face.

"You just cannot hide your true self from me, as real breeding will always come through, my dear."

He grabbed her hand and examined it.

"As I suspected – not a day's hard work has ever blighted this tiny hand," he sighed, kissing it lightly.

Temia withdrew her hand as if it had been scalded.

"Sir Thomas – " she breathed, turning scarlet.

"Come, you can trust me with your secret. What is it – you have run away from your Mama and Papa to avoid an unhappy alliance?"

Her shocked face told him all he needed to know.

"Ah, I thought as much. What was it – they wanted you to marry some old oaf to keep the family silver intact? Or was it a business deal to enrich your father?"

Temia's eyes filled with tears.

She looked into his kind face and immediately felt she could tell him everything.

"It is true. I have run away from an undesirable match, a hateful man whom I despise, but who is holding my father to ransom.

"The bounder! Who is this fiend? If I know him, I swear I shall go and give the man a piece of my mind!"

"Lord Alphonse," admitted Temia.

Sir Thomas threw his head back and sighed deeply.

"Oh, that brute! So, he's up to his old tricks again. He should have had his fingers burned enough after the last time he attempted such fraud. Temia, you do know that the man has a wife?"

"I did not," replied Temia aghast. "Then, what he is trying to do is illegal!"

"Exactly."

"Why has this not come to light previously?"

"Lord Alphonse is a very powerful man – he is very effective at silencing all his opponents. The reason I found out about his crimes is that I rescued a servant of his, who had been beaten to within an inch of his life. I took him home and gradually helped him out of his predicament."

"You mean he tried to kill his own servant?"

"Yes. The boy had discovered the existance of his wife, who is locked up in a lunatic asylum near London. Lord Alphonse had just announced an 'engagement' when the boy, whom he had ill-treated, threatened to go to the Police. In response he tried to kill him. When I found the poor lad, he was so frightened, it was three weeks before he would even tell me his name."

"The devil! He must be stopped!"

"As I said, Temia, he has friends in high places and does not think twice about resorting to violence to obtain what he wants. Did he threaten your father?"

"Not with violence, but blackmail. He discovered a family secret and threatened to spread it to ruin my father's reputation."

"Then, we must go at once to the Police and have him stopped!"

"No, please, I cannot," pleaded Temia. "I don't wish this to be dragged through the newspapers as it will only hurt Mama. It is best if we allow matters to rest. He will let them be now that I am no longer at home."

"But you have run away from your family and all because of this bounder!"

"Please – it is what I want."

"Very well," he answered, "but if you change your mind, then you must let me know. A woman on her own cannot take on this kind of brute without help. It is there if you wish it. Now, I ask if you will dine with me after the show tonight. Wentworth may join us, so I hope you will not mind. But do say you will, Temia."

She hesitated.

"The Earl of Wentworth?" she asked him, as coolly as she could. Even so, just the mere mention of his name caused her heart to beat faster.

"Yes, I am afraid I have to keep my eye on him. He has not been himself since his father died and is prone to unfortunate outbursts that need a calming hand."

"Then, I accept."

"And you will not mind if we are not alone?"

"Not at all," replied Temia, smiling. "Now, I really must return to my work, if you will excuse me."

He raised his hat and lifted her hand to his lips.

"Until this evening, then," he sighed in a tone that left Temia in no doubt of his feelings for her.

*

After the show that evening, Temia found herself disappointed that the Earl did not make an appearance.

Sir Thomas explained, as they rode in his carriage to *Claridge's* for supper, that he had a headache and so had remained at his London house.

"It's just as well as the last time we went there, he embroiled himself in a heated discussion about politics and we were asked to leave."

"Is he a violent man?" she asked, keen to discover more about him.

"No, I would not say that. But his temper is on a hair trigger of late. It will cause him much harm one day."

Temia enjoyed a delicious supper at *Claridge's* and Sir Thomas drove her back to Mrs. Hook's in his carriage.

Ever the gentleman, he simply kissed her hand at the door and left, promising to see her the next evening.

*

The weeks whirled by and Temia found so much to occupy herself with at the theatre.

At first Sophia had not asked her questions about her father, but later she enquired more about him. Temia was wise not to reveal the family's real surname.

"Lord Morris – tell me more of him," Sophia would say and somehow it did not feel as if it was her father they were talking about.

Sir Thomas regularly took her to dinner.

Sometimes Sophia would join them and make up a foursome and on these occasions, the Earl would sit in the corner, not saying much, but even so Temia could feel his eyes always on her and not Sophia.

She often tried to draw him into the conversation and, for a few moments, he would speak and, then, would fall silent and brooding once more.

"That Earl's not too much fun," remarked Sophia. "Perhaps he thinks too much of himself to bother with the likes of us!"

"No, it's not that. His father died last year and he is still grieving."

"Well, I don't think I care to come to dinner again if he is going to be so difficult. Next time, ask Lily – she'd be thrilled to be seen out with a Lord."

Upstairs in their room, Sophia helped Temia take off her dress.

"Temia, I am going to visit Mrs. Sebright tomorrow afternoon. Would you care to come with me?"

Temia paused.

Though she was not entirely sure that she believed in the whole idea of spiritualism, she was intrigued by it.

And, if there was any method of conversing with Jasper, then, had she not said she would try it?

Sophia was eagerly awaiting an answer and finally, Temia relented.

"Very well, I will come with you."

"Good, you will not be disappointed. Mrs. Sebright is a wonderful woman. I swear to God, the last time I was there, it was not her face I was looking at when Mama spoke to me through her – but my own dear Mama's!"

Temia did not feel inclined to believe such notions, but she was still very keen to hear something from Jasper.

So when, the next afternoon, Sophia took her in a Hackney cab to a house in Dover Street, in spite of herself, she suddenly felt distinctly nervous.

Sophia rang the bell as they waited on the doorstep.

A maid in a white cap opened the door.

"Have you ladies come for the seance?" she asked. "Please come this way."

Temia did not know what she had expected, but the house seemed very ordinary inside.

They were shown into a back parlour with a large circular table in the centre. It looked very much as if it were about to be laid for tea and *not* a seance.

Presently, they were joined by two other ladies and then, an elderly gentleman and a younger man whom he introduced as his nephew.

"What happens now?" whispered Temia.

"Well, normally, Mrs. Sebright comes in and talks to us and then she goes into a trance."

Then a tall woman in flowing robes walked in and every movement she made was graceful and deliberate, almost as if she was on a stage.

Her long red hair flowed loosely down her back and was held in place by a folded scarf around her forehead.

She sat down at the table.

"I can feel the spirits around me – " she sighed.

She looked round the table and saw Temia.

"You have not been here before, have you, young lady?" she asked, fixing Temia with her golden eyes.

"No, it is my first time," she answered nervously.

"We shall say a prayer and join hands. Then if there is a spirit who wishes to speak to someone here, he or she will make themselves known to me. Through me, they will speak. Don't be afraid, they will not harm you. All I ask is that no one leaves the room before the seance has ended."

Sophia took Temia's hand and squeezed it.

Mrs. Sebright closed her eyes and lifted her face up to Heaven. She said a prayer and then, raising her voice, she exhorted the spirits to come close. She then stared into the middle distance and concentrated on an invisible spot.

All the while, her assistant, a younger woman who had entered the room during the prayer, stood by waiting.

Temia watched fascinated as she muttered under her breath. All of a sudden, she sat bolt upright and rolled her eyes up into her head.

"*Jarvis, Jarvis!*" she growled, her voice becoming masculine and rasping. "*Why did you not take Bessie to the country as I asked?*"

The elderly gentleman turned pale.

"Are you Jarvis?" asked the assistant.

"Yes," whispered the man, hoarsely. Temia could see that he was quite clearly agitated.

"*This is Horace! Take Bessie to the country, she's too old to be in the town!*" bellowed Mrs. Sebright, her features creasing and contorting.

"Can you understand?" asked the assistant.

The old man nodded.

"Horace is my dear brother and Bessie is his horse. Horace! I will have her sent to the estate in Camberley at once!" he shouted.

"Good, good," muttered Mrs. Sebright. "There are more spirits – there's a young man who wants to speak, but he is shy. '*Is my sister here*?' he keeps saying."

The assistant looked around the room.

"Is there anyone here with a brother on the other side?" she asked, searching each face intently.

Temia felt her stomach turn over.

What if it *was* Jasper?

She could not move or speak. She did not believe in such things after all – it could not be true!

"My friend does," piped up Sophia, "but she's shy."

Mrs. Sebright bowed her head for a moment and, when she lifted it, Temia gasped out loud for her face was transformed into the smooth features of a young man.

She recognised at once the sensitive expression and soft curve of his cheek.

"*My little Tia. You must warn our father – he is in great danger! This man, the Lord, who is blackmailing him, will stop at nothing! Your flight has been in vain.*"

"What can I do?" cried Temia out loud.

She half-rose out of her chair, eyes staring wildly and tears coursing down her cheeks.

"Please sit down, miss – Mrs. Sebright cannot have the circle broken," called the assistant. "You must address the young man directly if you seek an answer."

"Jasper – darling, is that you?" quavered Temia.

"*It is, my dear sister,*" came the disembodied voice.

It was as faint as the wind in the trees – almost a half-whisper.

"*The evidence lies in Hanwell,*" it continued, "*the man who told you this spoke the truth, but it is not he you will marry, even though he has marriage in mind. No, you will in the end wed the one whose pain will cause him to mortally wound his best friend!*"

Suddenly, Mrs. Sebright began to breathe rapidly and noisily. Her chest then heaved and she appeared to be feeling a terrible pain. A low moan issued from her mouth and she slumped forward in her chair.

Like a flash, her assistant ran forward with a bottle of smelling salts in her hand.

"Give her air! No more messages today! She has exhausted herself."

A low murmur of disappointment went up and the other sitters rose from their chairs.

Temia sat rooted to hers with her hands gripping the side of it so hard that her knuckles were turning white.

"Please stay behind," said the assistant coming over to her and Sophia. "Mrs. Sebright will want to talk to you shortly. I have never seen such a transfiguration before – the likeness of a young man! Was he your brother?"

"Yes," muttered Temia, still deep in shock, "he was – killed in the Crimea – five years ago.

"That is why it took such effort for Mrs. Sebright to bring him forth. War heroes are very taxing on her energy. It's the manner of their passing, you see – if they go during battle, it takes so much for them to come through."

"Are you all right?" asked Sophia, taking Temia's hand. "I can ask for brandy if it would help you."

"No, I will be fine in a moment."

Mrs. Sebright now regained consciousness and she rose from her chair and moved towards Temia.

"My dear," she began, "it's been a long time since I experienced such a dramatic appearance from any spirit. Your brother appeared so anxious to contact you – I hope you understood his message? I do confess, I don't recall a word, only the feeling that he was desperate to talk to you."

"It made perfect sense to me," responded Temia. "I am shaken as I did not expect anything so – lucid."

"Ah, my guides were working hard this afternoon. It must have been a matter of great significance for them to rally round and help the young man come through."

"How did you know it was him?" asked Sophia.

"When he called me 'Tia'. It was a pet name he called me when we were small. I would not have believed it had I not witnessed it for myself!"

Mrs. Sebright laughed.

"But my dear, it's the unbelievers who are always the easiest for me to work with. It's as if their resistance gives me strength and often wonderful and strange things happen. I have known physical material to be produced in such circumstances!"

"Physical material?" asked Temia.

"You mean trumpets and such like," asked Sophia.

"Yes, my dear. I do."

Mrs. Sebright laid her hand on Temia's.

"You must come again, Miss – ?"

"Morris."

"I shall look forward to our next meeting. Now, I must go off and rest as the spirits have drained me. Good afternoon, ladies!"

With that she swept out of the room.

Temia and Sophia stared after her, watching her flowing skirts swirl around her like foam on the tide.

Later, when they were comfortably ensconced in a nearby tearoom, Temia found it impossible to speak.

'Jasper echoed just what Sir Thomas told me,' she thought to herself. 'If only I could find this lunatic asylum, then perhaps Papa will have a chance of dispensing with Lord Alphonse for good. With the right evidence, he would bring the full power of the law down on his head!'

She did not confide her thoughts in Sophia – no, she would not involve her in the whole sorry affair.

'I will ask Sir Thomas to tell me more of what he knows,' she decided. 'I shall have to trust him.'

Sophia and Temia did not discuss it again until later that evening. Temia was making up Sophia's face when she brought up the subject.

"Temia, what should we now do to help our Papa? What if all that Mrs. Sebright said was true? Should we not do something to prevent him from coming to harm?"

Temia had yet to tell Sophia the true reason for her flight from home.

"I have still to decide on my course of action," said Temia. "But rest assured, I intend to discover more."

After the show, Sir Thomas was waiting for her in his carriage. She climbed in and felt a distinct pang of disappointment to find that the Earl was not with him.

Much later after a delightful meal, Temia said that she was tired and wished to return home.

As the carriage drew up outside Mrs. Hook's, Sir Thomas took her hand and kissed it fervently.

Then, he put his arm round her and drew her close.

Temia passively allowed him to enfold her. It was the first time he had done so, but it was not repulsive.

"My darling," he sighed, holding her even closer.

Before she realised what was happening, his mouth was on hers and he was kissing her.

At first gently and then more insistently.

Temia pulled away – although she was very fond of him, she did not wish him to kiss her in such a way.

"Temia," he murmured, gazing into her eyes. "You must know I care for you a great deal."

She could not look at him. Instead she dropped her eyes in a gesture she hoped he would construe as modest.

"I am fond of you too," she replied, "but now, I am very tired and must go. Goodnight, Sir Thomas, and thank you for dinner."

She quickly left the carriage and, at Mrs. Hook's door, she turned and quickly waved before going inside.

She caught her breath. Her heart was pounding, but not through excitement. Rather, it was the knowledge that Sir Thomas was trying to tell her that he was in love with her and she knew that she did not return his love.

No, it was the vision of another who haunted her dreams so frequently.

'Sooner or later I will be forced to tell him I do not love him,' she thought. 'But I must stay my hand until I have discovered the truth about Lord Alphonse.'

Even so, in her heart she yearned to see the Earl of Wentworth again.

'But how to break it to Sir Thomas?' she agonised. '*His best friend*!'

The very thought tore her in two – how could she come between two such good friends?

CHAPTER SIX

Sir Thomas did not come to the theatre the next evening. Instead he sent a note of apology along with an orchid in a box.

"No beau this evening? quizzed Sophia.

"He has been detained at a meeting in the City."

"He must be very clever."

"Yes, he is."

"And he has quite an eye for you! He does know that you're from a fine family, doesn't he?"

"I have told him just a little of my circumstances."

"So, there's no obstacle should he propose!"

"Only that I don't want to marry him – "

Sophia looked at their reflection in the mirror to see that Temia was blushing.

"It's his friend, isn't it – the one who rarely speaks? I've seen his eyes on you and yours on his. Oh, to have two men in love with me like that!"

Temia moved quickly away, horrified that she had shown her feelings so transparently.

She did not pass comment on what Sophia had said, but then could it be true? Dare she hope that the Earl could have feelings for her?

She busied herself with the make-up box and soon, Sophia was rushing off to go on stage.

As soon as the dressing room had cleared, she sat down and stared at her reflection in the mirror.

'Do I love him?' she questioned herself.

Almost as soon as she allowed herself that thought, there came a soft knocking on the door.

Believing it to be the boy who had been helping her, she opened it without looking to see who was there.

With her back to the door, she called out,

"If you've finished clearing up, Albert, can you go and tell Mr. Baker I'll be finished tomorrow afternoon?"

"Much as I would love to clear up for you, Temia, I don't think I am suitably attired!" came a deep rich voice.

Temia whirled round, and gasped in shock as she saw that it was not Albert, but *the Earl of Wentworth*.

"Oh, please forgive me, my Lord – I thought it was Albert, my assistant."

The Earl laughed and Temia was struck at how a smile transformed his face. He was handsome anyway, but smiling, he was stunningly so.

Her heart beat alarmingly fast and she felt herself short of breath as she looked at him.

He had taken off his hat and was now perched upon one of the long benches that served as a dressing table.

"Thomas has been detained," he started, "and so, I thought you may care to join me for dinner this evening."

Temia hesitated.

Her heart was saying yes, but her head was saying something different.

Although there was no formal arrangement that she was Sir Thomas's sweetheart, she felt a degree of loyalty towards him.

"I – am – busy," she stuttered, after a long silence.

It hurt to refuse him, but this was Sir Thomas's best friend.

"Of course, you are loyal to Thomas. Very well, I shall not trouble you further this evening, but will see you another time with him."

Underneath the politeness, Temia could sense his hurt, as if she herself had been pierced by a spear.

She had just refused the man she loved!

He raised his hat and left as quietly as he had come.

Temia put on her cloak and then left at once for Mrs. Hook's – she did not care that she was meant to help the girls undress later, they would manage for themselves.

Arriving back at her lodgings, she ran upstairs and threw herself on the bed in a flood of tears.

She cried herself to sleep, still wearing her clothes, much to Sophia's surprise when she came in much later.

*

Leo Baker carefully examined the new backdrop and declared himself to be a delighted man.

"Excellent! You have done a wonderful job!"

"Thank you, Mr. Baker," answered Temia, full of pleasure in having successfully completed her task.

"You can stay with *Les Jolies Mademoiselles* for as long as you wish. Furthermore, I shall pay you a salary from now on. Come to my office a bit later. I don't want another theatre snapping you up, as once word gets around that I have the best scenery designer in London, they will all want you! Well done, my dear. Very well done."

Temia supervised the loading of the backdrop onto the waiting cart and then went into the Green Room, the rest room for the girls of *Les Jolies Mademoiselles.*

She picked up a copy of *The Times* and sat down to read it. She liked to scan the *Court Circular* so that she at least felt a little part of the world she had scarcely had a chance to inhabit.

She turned to the pages at the back and just then something in the *Notices* section caught her eye.

"*Missing*." it read. "*Anxious parents eagerly seek news of their daughter, Miss Temia Brandon of Bovendon Hall, Northamptonshire. Fair hair, blue eyes and slim build. Anyone knowing about a person of that description, please contact Box 34.*"

She read it with a lump in her throat. So her parents were now trying to find her!

Tears sprang to her eyes. Her first instinct was to write to the box number anonymously and say that she was well, but that she did not wish to be found.

'But what if they are trying to contact me to tell me that Lord Alphonse has left them alone?'

She was still crying over the newspaper when Leo Baker came into the Green Room looking for her.

"Now then, what's all this?" he remarked gently in a voice that was so different from his usual hearty manner.

He put his arm protectively around Temia and attempted to comfort her.

Quickly she folded the newspaper so he could not read the notice – but it was too late, he had already caught a glimpse of it.

"Why do you not just write to your parents and let them know you are all right?" he suggested. "You don't have to tell them your whereabouts. In any case, we are about to move out of Kensington to Covent Garden."

"I cannot!" she cried, burying her face in her skirt.

"Well, perhaps write to your mother? If there has been some argument, then at least write to her. But now, the cart is here, Temia, you are needed out front."

Temia dried her eyes and, as she was organising the removal of the backdrop, she came to a decision.

'I shall write to Mama at once – she has not had a single word from me since the first note I sent. There is no need to tell her too much, just that I am well and happy and if there is good news, put another notice in *The Times.*'

Now that the backdrop had been painted, she was free until the evening – the last performance of the season at the *Royal Kent Theatre.*

Sophia was just leaving when Temia arrived back at Mrs. Hook's. She had packed most of her things and a trunk stood at the end of her bed and Temia almost tripped over it as she entered the room.

"Oh, I am sorry!" apologised Sophia. "I wanted to make ready for leaving tomorrow. I'm always so behind and you left so early this morning."

"The Earl came to the theatre yesterday and asked me to dine with him after the show."

"And you accepted, I hope?"

"No, I could not. Oh, Sophia, how could I when I know that his best friend has feelings for me? Even though we have not made promises to each other, it would have been disloyal for me to have dined with him alone."

"Is that why you were still dressed and fast asleep, when I came back last night?"

Temia nodded.

"And then, today, I found a notice in *The Times* that Mama and Papa are seeking news of me."

"Will you write to them?"

"I have decided to write a letter to Mama. She will understand more why I write secretly. Papa will not."

"Then, I will leave you be. Will I see you at the theatre this evening? It's the last performance."

"You will," answered Temia, taking off her cloak.

As soon as Sophia had left, she took up a sheet of paper and a quill pen and began to write.

She posted her letter that afternoon.

'There, it's done,' she sighed.

She felt a sense of relief as she walked towards the theatre. The lights were already on when she arrived and once inside she was stopped by the stage door manager.

"Something's come for you," he grunted.

He went into his little office and emerged carrying a huge bunch of flowers.

Temia's heart skipped a beat.

Could they be from the Earl? She prayed that they were, but in her heart she knew that they were from Sir Thomas.

She opened the attached note and read,

"*I look forward to supper later at Henri's. I will be at the stage door at ten with my carriage.*

Affectionately yours, Thomas."

The show was a tremendous success that evening. The girls received endless curtain calls as Temia watched from the wings with a tear in her eye.

She was so proud to be even a small part of this wonderful show!

"Come and take a bow with me, Temia!" cried Leo Baker, taking her hand and pulling her onto the stage.

Before she could protest, she found herself under the burning lights, bowing with *Les Jolies Mademoiselles* to thunderous applause.

Awkward at first, she soon became accustomed to the roar of the crowd and took her bows with the others.

"Is that Temia? No, it *cannot* be!"

The blonde young woman in the stalls cried out to her companion and almost fainted from shock.

"What is it, Georgiana. Do you feel ill?"

Georgiana leaned forward and looked again.

"Yes, it is! Oh, my word. So this is where she has been hiding! I should have guessed she might run away to the theatre. But what is she doing here? And so close?"

Her puzzled friend waited with her until the crowds had gone and then accompanied her to the stage door.

"I shall ask to see her – and I will not be put off!"

"Who is that girl?" her friend asked Georgiana.

"My missing cousin! Her mother is so frantic with worry and she has been right under our noses all this time!"

Georgiana strode up to the stage door and knocked on it. The stage door manager peered out and was taken aback to see two young ladies of obvious gentility.

"Yes, miss?"

"I have come for Miss Brandon. She works here."

"No lady of that name at this theatre, miss. You are mistaken."

"But I have just seen her here – on the stage!"

"I'm sorry, miss, I say again, you're mistaken!"

"Miss Temia Brandon! She's here, I know."

The stage door manager thought for a second.

"There's a Miss Temia Morris, but you've only just missed her. Her young man collected her ten minutes ago."

"Oh! How unfortunate! I really must contact her. Is there an address where I can write to her?"

"Well, they all moves on tomorrow, but here is the address of her lodgings."

Georgiana handed him a shilling.

"Why, thank you, miss!" he touched his forelock.

"I know what I must do," she said, as she climbed in to her carriage, "as soon as I arrive home, I will write to Aunt Alice and tell her I have found Temia."

"Perhaps she does not wish to be found," suggested her friend quizzically.

"That is of no importance," answered Georgiana. "Aunt Alice must know – and as soon as possible!"

*

The jet-black carriage rumbled over the cobbles of Mayfair. Inside, Sir Thomas Babbington was holding the hand of Temia Brandon and stroking it gently.

"I want this evening to be so special, my dove," he crooned, gazing into her eyes. "Henri is expecting us and has promised me the best table in the house."

"What is the occasion?" she asked excitedly. "Did your meeting go well in the City?"

"It did, but that is not the reason we are going to visit Monsieur Henri's establishment. I have an important matter I wish to discuss with you."

Temia's face fell.

"Is something amiss?" she asked.

Sir Thomas chuckled.

"Don't you worry your head with such concerns, my angel. I don't intend to give too much away, as I know how much you adore surprises."

Monsieur Henri's was located in a small side street off Park Lane and was considered very fashionable.

"You will like it here," insisted Sir Thomas, as a waiter showed them to their table in a secluded corner.

As soon as they were seated in the plush dining room, Monsieur Henri himself came to greet them.

"Sir Thomas. How wonderful to see you and who is this charming young lady?"

"Henri, this is Miss Morris, a dear friend of mine."

"*Très belle, très jolie!*" exclaimed Monsieur Henri. "*Enchanté, mademoiselle.* You will drink champagne, of course, and I have a very special bottle on ice for you."

He clapped his hands and a silver bucket full of ice was brought to the table and he then opened the bottle.

With that and a quick wink to Sir Thomas, he made a short bow and then left the table.

"Do you like the restaurant?" asked Sir Thomas.

"Very much, thank you."

"To you, my dearest!" he murmured, raising his glass with a smile.

Temia followed suit and took a sip from her glass.

"Is it to your taste?"

"It's most delicious, Sir Thomas, but can we order something to eat?" asked Temia, taking another sip. "I shall get a headache if I drink this without food."

He snapped his fingers and a waiter appeared.

"Two *steak entrecôte*, please," he ordered.

Temia and Sir Thomas chatted away until the food arrived and then, she drank some more champagne.

As she set it down, she noticed there was something sparkling in the bottom of her glass.

"Oh, what can it be?" she said, picking it up and examining it.

"I thought you would never notice, my love!"

Temia dipped her finger into the liquid and pulled out a diamond ring.

"Oh!" she cried, holding it up to the light.

"Yes, my darling. I want you to marry me. Temia, will you? I love you so very much and want nothing more than to spend the rest of my life with you."

"So there you are!" came a sudden voice. "I have searched all over Mayfair for you!"

Temia looked up to see the Earl standing there, gesturing to a waiter to bring another chair to the table.

"Wentworth!"

"I missed you at the theatre. So, I went to the Club and had a few drinks, but you not did appear."

"Wentworth, old boy. I am having a private dinner with Temia. In fact, I have just asked her to marry me!"

The Earl froze in his chair.

His face fell and took on a wounded expression for a fleeting moment.

Temia watched while he composed himself. He sat upright and then jumped up and stormed off to the door.

"Richard!" yelled Sir Thomas. "Temia, my darling. I am sorry. I should go after him. Will you excuse me?"

Temia breathed a sigh of relief.

As she held the sparkling ring up to the light, she twirled it around and examined the large central diamond.

'It's beautiful,' she sighed, 'but I cannot accept. If I needed proof of the man I love, then I have just received it. My heart left the room at the same time as the Earl.'

When Sir Thomas eventually returned, he seemed very upset. His hair was awry and his face red.

"I'm very sorry, Temia, but I have lost my appetite. Would you mind if we left? I have just asked Monsieur to fetch our cloaks."

"Not at all, Thomas, but what has happened? You look terrible!"

"It's Wentworth. There was an argument and he bally-well went for me."

Temia did not need any further explanation. She knew exactly what had transpired between the two men.

She did not speak until they were in the carriage.

She had been holding onto the ring since he had returned to their table, and now, she returned it to him.

"I am sorry, but I cannot accept your proposal," she whispered.

"But why?"

"I-I – "

"You are upset – I do understand, my darling. It was Wentworth's outburst, was it not?"

Temia nodded her head. It was not a lie, after all.

Outside her lodgings, the carriage came to a halt.

"Goodnight, Thomas," she said, kissing his cheek.

She was relieved that he was clearly still too upset to attempt to kiss her lips again.

He stared at Temia with such love that she felt tears rise to her eyes.

She knew, however, without a shadow of doubt that she did not love him.

*

Temia slept late the next day – and it was fortunate that she and Sophia did not have to leave Mrs Hook's until late afternoon.

The cab came at two o'clock for their luggage and then they went back upstairs to finish clearing their room.

"Where is the duster?" asked Temia. "Mrs. Hook will be cross if we don't leave the room spick and span."

"I'll go and ask her for it," offered Sophia.

Ten minutes later she returned with a strange look on her face and no feather duster.

"Temia, this letter has just come for you."

She handed it to her and, at once, Temia saw that it bore her mother's handwriting.

"So soon!" she whispered.

"She must have replied at once. Do you think she is in London for it to have arrived so swiftly?"

Temia's hands were shaking as she read the letter.

"She is coming to London tomorrow! Oh, how did she find out where I was? I don't understand! Wait – she says that Cousin Georgiana saw me on stage last night and sent her a letter that she must have received this morning. The stage doorman gave her this address."

"Oh, Temia! What else does she say?"

"Papa does not know of this, but she wishes to meet me at two o'clock in Fortnum and Mason's restaurant. Oh, Sophia! What shall I do?"

"You must see your Mama, of course."

"But what if she brings Papa with her and they then attempt to drag me back to Northamptonshire?"

"Do you really believe that could happen?"

Temia sat down on the bed and sighed with despair.

"Sophia, I confess I don't know."

Just then, the heavy footsteps of Mrs. Hook could be heard coming up the stairs.

"Mrs. Hook! She will be wanting her keys back!"

Temia tucked the letter into the waistband of her skirt, as the carriage was ready to go to Covent Garden.

'Tomorrow,' she thought. 'I shall decide tomorrow morning what to do for the best.'

As she closed the door behind her, she could not help but wonder what the next few days would bring.

CHAPTER SEVEN

Their new lodgings were a tall house tucked away just off the Strand. Although the area was not as smart as Kensington, Mrs. Timms kept a clean house and was not as bad-tempered as Mrs. Hook.

The troupe arrived in fits and starts and, as Sophia and Temia were the last to turn up, they got the attic room.

"It's not as nice as our old place," remarked Sophia. "There's barely enough room to do a pirouette! Mr. Baker wants us at the theatre at half-past two. What time has he asked for you, Temia?"

"Ten o'clock. He wishes me to help organise the scenery. He mentioned that there might be more to do."

"Lord!" cried Sophia, "not another dance?"

Just then Mrs. Timms put her head round the door.

"Sorry to disturb you, ladies, but is one of you Miss Temia Morris?"

"I am," answered Temia. "What is it?"

"This came for you earlier. A very fine seal it has too, look – "

Temia recognised at once it was from Sir Thomas, as she took the letter gingerly from Mrs. Timms.

"Aren't you going to open it?" Sophia asked her eagerly. "Which one is it from?"

"Sir Thomas. I do hope he's not angry with me for refusing his proposal."

"The girls all say it makes a gentleman keener if you refuse him."

Temia took a deep breath and broke the seal on the letter. What she found filled her with a sense of relief.

"He says he has been forced to return to his estate to deal with an urgent matter and so he will not be seeing me for the next few evenings. He will send word when he intends to return."

"And so, the way is now well and truly clear for the Earl of Wentworth!" added Sophia mischievously.

Temia blushed as she refolded the letter.

She had to admit relief that Sit Thomas was going to be absent for the next few evenings and Sophia was right – if the Earl was to make an appearance this time, would she be able to refuse any invitation he may care to offer?

Blowing out the candle, she settled for the night.

'*Oh, Richard*!' she sighed to herself, hoping with every inch of her being that the Earl would come to the theatre to see her.

*

Temia went to *The Olympic Theatre* early the next day to supervise the scenery and then asked Leo Baker if she might slip away for a few hours.

"Family business," she explained.

"You are not thinking of leaving us, I hope! That would never do – *never*!"

"No, I am very happy where I am."

As soon as she had finished her duties, Temia left to walk to Fortnum's in Piccadilly. Pushing open the pale-green doors, Temia quickly made her way up the stairs to the restaurant on the fourth floor.

Her heart was in her mouth as she emerged from the staircase.

Her Mama was standing by a podium, waiting for her. As soon as she saw her daughter, tears filled her eyes and she held out her arms to her.

"Temia darling!" she called, flying towards her.

They embraced for a while and then Mama said,

"Come, there is a table waiting for us."

Temia sat down and took her mother's hand in hers.

"Mama, it is so good to see you. How is Papa?"

"If the truth be known, he is a changed man."

"And Lord Alphonse, does he still trouble you?"

"I am afraid he does, darling. More so than before, if anything. When you disappeared, he was furious! He sent out search parties for you, convinced that you had fled abroad. He had his men combing the ports for any sign of you. Had he found you – "

"But he did not, thank God."

"If he knew you were here, he would make a great deal of trouble for you. He has underestimated your ability to survive away from the bosom of your family. Going to school in Paris has made you an independent woman.

"You are well, Temia? You look just as beautiful as ever."

"Very well, thank you," she replied, "and happy!"

"I confess I was very troubled when Georgiana said that you were working in a *theatre*. I had always believed that only loose women went on the stage."

"But, I am not on the stage. I paint the scenery and the girls' faces. They are nothing like I had thought – they are not loose women at all!"

"But theatricals have such lax morals, Temia, tell me, dearest, you have not – fallen, have you?"

"Goodness, Mama! I am shocked you should think such a thing! I can assure you that my virtue is intact."

"I am sorry to speak frankly, but I am so worried."

"I am more concerned about you and Papa," replied Temia, nibbling on a sandwich, "you said that he was a changed man. What did you mean by that?"

Her Mama took a deep breath.

"Lord Alphonse has taken his revenge in an awful way. He has been taking horses without paying for them and is ruining your father. We live in constant fear that he will broadcast your father's secret to all and sundry just out of spite. Now that he knows you are out of his reach, he has become bitter and even more unpleasant than ever. All this has made your Papa terribly depressed."

"Oh, Mama. I am so sorry I had to leave you and Papa, but I was left with no choice. I could not marry Lord Alphonse and what is more, I have discovered that he was not in a position to offer me marriage anyway."

"What do you mean?"

"He is already married."

"Impossible! How do you know this to be true?"

"A friend of mine. I confided in him the reason why I ran away from home and he said that he knew for a fact that Lord Alphonse has a wife already."

"Then, why has no one ever seen her?"

"He has had her committed to a lunatic asylum in Middlesex."

"And this friend, he is certain of his information?"

"Mama, he would not lie to me and then, something wonderful happened. Oh, Mama! I have had a message from Jasper!"

Lady Brandon turned white and began to cry.

"Don't say such things, Temia. Or you will really upset me."

"But Mama, I saw it with my own eyes! I went to a spiritualist – Mrs. Sebright – and Jasper came through! He told me that the evidence lies in Hanwell – that is where Lady Alphonse is imprisoned."

"I don't believe it, why would he do such a thing?"

"You have said yourself that he is slowly extorting money from Papa and ruining him, that would be why."

"But how can we prevent him? If I thought for one moment that what you say is true and that he has a wife, then we could bring in the law."

Temia paused, a scheme forming in her head.

"Mama, supposing we visited the asylum and took our Solicitor with us? With a sworn affidavit to the effect that he has a wife who still lives, then perhaps he will leave the family alone!"

Lady Brandon stirred her tea and thought.

"If I believed for a moment that there was a way to get rid of that dreadful man – "

"Mama, the only way we can discover whether or not it is true is to go and see for ourselves."

"Surely, but running off to some lunatic asylum, Temia, it is just *not* done."

"And neither is blackmail and extortion! But that does not prevent Lord Alphonse from pursuing Papa."

"Then, there is only one course of action and that is to do as you suggest. I will do all in my power to stop him and so I am prepared to come with you to Hanwell."

"Oh, Mama! Thank you! Thank you! Will you be able to stay in London for a few days longer?"

"I will write to your Papa and tell him that I have been taken ill with a cold. I shall go to Marianne and ask her if I may stay with her."

"And our Solicitor?"

"I will make an appointment to see Mr. Burleigh first thing tomorrow."

A clock chimed and Temia realised she had to go.

"Mama, I must leave you. There is still so much to do at the theatre."

"Where can I write to you, darling?"

"This is the address of my lodgings but, please, don't visit me. It's not – as you would wish."

"Darling, I am so glad we have met and spoken. I have been beside myself with worry ever since you left."

They rose and walked downstairs to the street.

"And I am sorry I could not tell you where I was. I believed that if you found out, you would surely send Lord Alphonse to fetch me."

"Last week, perhaps I would have done, but now, I am just thankful I have seen you, well and, I hope, happy."

"Yes, I am, Mama, but there is something else that I would discuss with you."

Lady Brandon stopped and turned quite pale.

"What is it, my darling? I don't think I could take more bad news!"

"Not bad news, but *strange* news. The young lady I share my room with – she is none other than Papa's long-lost daughter."

"With that woman?"

"Yes, Mama. But she is nice and not at all rough."

"And you are certain that she is – ?"

"My half-sister? Yes. She has shown me a letter written to her mother from Papa. I would recognise the hand anywhere."

"And her mother?"

"She was an actress, as we had heard, but the rest of the rumour was not true. Sophia's mother died without a husband and died refusing to name Sophia's father."

Lady Brandon now composed herself and resumed walking along Piccadilly. She held her head high and, if she was upset at this news, she did not show it.

"Has she asked to meet her father?"

"Not exactly, but she desires it, I know."

"We shall have to deal with this another time, at the moment my main concern is how to bring Lord Alphonse to justice."

At Leicester Square, Temia kissed her Mama and bade her farewell.

"Mama, you will write to me very soon and we will visit Hanwell to find out the truth for ourselves?"

"I promise you, we shall. Goodbye, Temia darling. Pray we will uncover something to our advantage!"

Temia felt a lump rising in her throat as she waved goodbye to her mother.

'Oh Lord!' she prayed, as she walked rapidly along the Strand, 'please let us find what we seek in Hanwell. Help bring the deceitful Lord Alphonse to justice.'

*

Opening night at *The Olympic Theatre* in Covent Garden was a tense affair. Leo Baker was in a terrible mood and shouted constantly at the girls before curtain up.

"He's been this way all day," whispered Sophia, as Temia was putting the finishing touches to some scenery.

"Shouted at us all the time during rehearsals. Oh, and you know who turned up looking for you this afternoon?"

Temia turned pale.

"Surely it was not Lord Alphonse?"

"Lord Alphonse? No, the one with the brooding eyes – the Earl of Wentworth."

"He came here?" asked Temia, feeling a little faint.

"Looking for you! At first he refused to believe you were not here and then said he'd return later."

"And Sir Thomas, was he with him?"

"No, he was not. Fortunately!"

"Sophia! Enough gossiping. Come to the front," roared Leo Baker.

Temia worked away at the scenery and tried not to think about the Earl. Her heart beat faster and she found it difficult to concentrate.

'Whatever the reason, it must be important. I hope he has not fallen out with Sir Thomas. If they both come tonight, there will be a great deal of trouble!'

Just before curtain up, Temia was busying herself with the last item of costume when there came a knock on the door and it was Hobson.

"Miss Temia, the Earl of Wentworth is at the stage door demandin' to see you. Shall I send him away? He seems awful vexed, so he does."

"No, I shall come out at once," she replied sighing.

Her heart was beating very fast as she approached the long corridor that led to the stage door.

She could see his silhouette outside in the street, wearing a top hat and a cape, as was his custom.

"Temia!" he called out, as he caught sight of her. "I feared you had disappeared."

"No, I have been occupied with family business," she answered. "What did you want?"

"Say you will dine with me this evening."

He looked at her with expectant and dark eyes. She wanted so much to accept, but felt that it was impossible, given the circumstances.

"I am afraid that I am not feeling well and intend to leave the theatre as soon as I can this evening," she replied, not looking at him.

She knew that if she looked into his eyes, then all would be lost. She would be powerless to resist him.

The Earl hung his head and nodded slowly.

"And I cannot persuade you otherwise?"

"Not tonight, I am sorry," she answered, feeling a strange aching sensation in her breast. How it hurt her to refuse him!

The performance was highly successful.

Les Jolies Mademoiselles caused a sensation with their new routines and even Temia had to admit that Lily sang like a bird.

But, even as the introduction to the last number was played, Temia was running backstage to collect her things.

She had seen Sir Thomas appear in a box just as the overture began and knew that he would encounter the Earl later at the stage door.

'It grieves me to leave without seeing him,' she thought as she left, 'but it's the only way!'

She almost did not care that Sir Thomas might be eager to see her after his absence, she simply did not want a confrontation between the two of them – with herself in the middle of it.

She soon made her way back to her new lodgings and undressed, put on her nightdress and waited for Sophia to return.

She wondered what had happened outside the stage door after the show. Would the Earl have come, in spite of her refusal to dine with him? And if he had, what words passed between him and his friend, Sir Thomas?

A long hour passed and eventually, Temia heard the sound of footsteps on the stairs outside.

Sophia opened the door and shook off her cloak.

"Heavens, it's raining so hard out there!" she cried, "you were wise to leave when you did, Temia."

"The Earl – did he wait at the stage door for me?"

"And Sir Thomas. You should have seen them! I swear if either of them had had a pistol, they would have shot each other!"

"They were arguing?"

"Like I've never heard gentlemen in public before! The Earl threatened to knock the blazes out of Sir Thomas and it was Hobson who stood between them and calmed them down or else blood would have been drawn."

"Was it because of me?"

"Well, first of all, the Earl rolled up, bold as you like and demanded to see you and you had left. Then along comes Sir Thomas, who accused him of 'sly behaviour'. The Earl flew into a towering rage and said all kinds of wicked things. And then, Sir Thomas lashed out at him!"

"He struck him?"

"Right on the chin! It was fortunate you weren't there, Temia. I hate to think what might have happened had you been present."

Temia bowed her head and tried to hide her tears. Although she had not accepted Sir Thomas's proposal, it rather assumed some kind of propriety over her.

And in her heart, she knew that she loved the Earl.

"What will you do?" asked Sophia, as she climbed into bed. "I have always I thought it would be nice to have two men in love with me, but after seeing the ugly scenes this evening, I don't think I would care for it one tiny bit."

"The Earl has not told me that he is in love with me," murmured Temia, wiping her eyes discreetly.

"But he is, as plain as day! But that temper of his – it's terrible!"

"He's still overwrought by the death of his father."

"He was like a man possessed! Temia, if he would strike his best friend, perhaps he would strike a lady."

"He would never do such a thing! He's troubled, that's all. He is not a violent man."

"How can you say so when you barely know him?"

"I know it in my heart, Sophia. I cannot explain it any better. Now, it is late and we must sleep."

Temia blew out her candle and settled down under the thin quilt. She could hear Sophia muttering her prayers under her breath.

Temia fell asleep, almost in spite of herself and she was soon dreaming of walking across green fields with the Earl and his arm was round her waist.

*

It was with relief that Temia noted that neither of them made an appearance at the theatre over the next few evenings.

Although in her heart, she yearned to see the Earl again, she contented herself with working as hard as she could, much to the approval of Leo Baker.

"A rise, a rise! That's what's needed!" he boomed, as he admired her latest piece of scenery.

"A rise?" enquired Temia, a little perplexed.

"In salary, of course! I am certain that it's not only the beautiful and talented *Les Jolies Mademoiselles* that are currently drawing the crowds. Did you know we are sold out for an entire week – *in advance*?"

"No, I did not." Temia was thrilled that she was held in such high esteem.

Sophia came rushing over to Temia almost as soon as Leo Baker had left her side.

"I never asked you. How was your mother?"

"I have persuaded her to come to Hanwell with me to see if Lady Alphonse exists."

"Did you mention me to her?"

"Yes, I did. Mama took it in her stride and did not make much comment."

After the show she lingered for a while, hoping that the Earl might be waiting outside for her, but as she went outside onto the wet and empty street, she realised with a sinking heart that he was not coming.

'Perhaps it's for the best,' she told herself, as she walked quickly back to the lodgings. 'But, oh, how I wish I was not so disappointed.'

*

Neither came for the next few evenings and Temia carried on as usual, but felt that her spirits were somewhat in decline.

Even Leo Baker firming up his offer of a rise did nothing to lift her.

Then, one afternoon, a letter arrived at the theatre.

Temia recognised at once her mother's handwriting and opened the letter quickly.

'It must be very important if she has gone to the trouble of having it delivered by hand,' she thought, as she unfolded it.

"Dearest Temia,

Mr. Burleigh has now been persuaded of the need for us to pay a visit to the asylum in Hanwell and has agreed to accompany us this afternoon.

I am sorry it is such short notice and hope you can be relieved of your duties. Please be ready at two o'clock sharp and I will collect you in a carriage,

Your own loving Mama."

"You are as white as a ghost, is something wrong?"

Sophia came up and put her hand on her shoulder.

"No, there is nothing wrong. Mama is taking me with the family Solicitor to Hanwell this afternoon."

"Oh, Lord!" cried Sophia, and then she covered her mouth, clearly embarrassed at sounding so common.

"I will go to Mr. Baker and ask his permission to return to Mrs. Timms's at once. I cannot go to the asylum wearing such shabby clothing."

"Good luck," whispered Sophia.

Fifteen minutes later, Temia was walking back to her lodgings.

She was frightened at what they might discover and was also conscious of not wasting Mr. Burleigh's time.

She wondered how her mother had persuaded the usually stern and forbidding Solicitor to accompany them.

And now, she was placing her trust in him, as well as her reputation. He surely would not take well to being subjected to her 'flight of female fancy' and, should Lady Alphonse not be in Hanwell or even exist, Temia did not like to consider how he might view her.

106

At two o'clock sharp she heard a carriage draw up and come to a halt outside the door of her lodgings.

Closing the front door behind her, Temia could see her Mama looking eagerly out of the window for her.

Next to her she could see the tall figure of Mr. Burleigh. Temia remembered well the full grey whiskers that sprouted like unruly rosemary bushes from either side of his face.

Climbing into the carriage, she sat opposite them.

Mr. Burleigh raised his hat and grunted a greeting.

"Temia, you will remember Mr. Burleigh?" said her Mama, "and he has something exciting to tell you."

Mr. Burleigh pursed his lips and began,

"Yes, Miss Brandon. You will be interested to hear that fate has conspired to throw a rather curious titbit in my direction. In fact, it is more than a titbit. Miss Brandon – I believe I have discovered something about Lord Alphonse that could put him in prison for a very long time!"

Temia gasped.

"You – believe – me?" she stuttered, an incredulous look spreading over her face.

"I confess that, at first, I may well have put it down to the overheated imaginings of the female brain had I not had an intriguing piece of information come my way this very morning. But first, we must uncover our evidence."

Mr. Burleigh hammered with his cane on the roof of the carriage and it lurched forward.

"Driver! To Hanwell and with all haste! Now," he said, settling down in his seat, "this morning I had a rather interesting visitor – "

CHAPTER EIGHT

Mr. Burleigh waited until they reached the outskirts of Hanwell before he spoke,

"This morning, the Duke of Weybridge came to see me and I confess that, until his visit, I was a little sceptical of your dear mother's motives in pursuing this man."

"But surely she explained that Lord Alphonse was blackmailing us?" asked Temia nervously.

"She did but, in my profession, until there is cast iron evidence, one tends to keep one's counsel. However, I digress. His Grace had come to ask advice on a personal matter. It now transpires that a certain Lord Alphonse is blackmailing his youngest sister. Of course, when I heard the name, it aroused my curiosity."

"What did he say?" asked Temia. "Do tell us!"

"My dear, it would seem that Lord Alphonse has made provision for you not reappearing and so made his approaches to Lady Hannah! He claimed to have evidence that the Duke had fathered a child by a dancer – which is quite untrue – and that he would reveal it to all and sundry, should she not comply."

"So, the Duke came straight to you?"

"The instant this character began to make threats. His Grace is not a man to be trifled with and would do anything to protect his good name."

"Did you mention that there was another instance of him attempting blackmail?"

"I did, and His Grace is very anxious to precipitate matters. I did not reveal, of course, that there was some evidence to suggest that Lord Alphonse's wife is still alive. I thought it best to wait until we have seen for ourselves."

Temia sat back and felt a glimmer of hope.

If the Duke was willing to prosecute, then, even if there was no Lady Alphonse, the mere fact that he was blackmailing others would be enough to secure an arrest.

Hanwell was a large but plain building surrounded by simple landscaping. Had Temia not known what it was, it could have been a rather austere country house.

The carriage came to a halt at the front entrance and they alighted.

"Mr. Warren is expecting us," said Mr. Burleigh to a man at the door, as he helped Lady Brandon up the steps.

Temia shuddered as they entered the tall hallway. A strong smell of carbolic soap rose into her nostrils along with another smell she could not identify.

As they arrived, a woman in a long black dress and white cap came towards them. Temia noticed a bunch of keys hanging from her belt. Her face was lined and her mouth turned downwards and she looked as if she did not know what it was to smile.

"Are you Lady Brandon's party?" she demanded without a hint of welcome.

"Yes, we are"

"Come with me. Mr. Warren is expecting you."

Temia clung to her Mama's arm as they walked along the echoing corridors with high ceilings. There were bars on the windows and the floors were highly polished.

From distant rooms came the sounds of moaning – Temia thought it sounded like a cow lowing rather than a human being.

She looked on in horror as they passed by an old woman who mimed knitting, even though she had neither needles nor wool in her hands.

They went up some stairs and then through a half-glazed door.

"Please wait here," they were instructed.

After a few moments, a door on the other side of the room opened and a small man with a hooked nose and thin hair plastered to his head came forward.

"Lady Brandon, I am Mr. Warren, the Governor – please come into my Office."

Temia rose from her chair and followed her mother and Mr. Burleigh. She felt terribly nervous and her heart beat rapidly underneath her cloak.

Mr. Warren indicated that they should sit on the chairs in front of his desk and they did so.

"What can I do for you, Lady Brandon?" asked Mr. Warren.

Temia thought that his eyes were rather cold. They were the kind of dirty grey that does not betray emotion.

"I believe that you have a certain woman here – her name is Lady Alphonse. For good reasons, it is imperative that I seek confirmation of her existence."

"Lady Alphonse? My Lady, as you will no doubt be aware, Hanwell is not an asylum for gentlefolk, but for persons of lesser means. Our inmates don't have a penny to their names, which is why they are here."

Temia had been expecting such an argument and had prepared herself for such an obstruction.

"Mr. Warren, I would not have come here had it not been of the utmost importance. I cannot impress upon you sufficiently how vital this is. Mr. Burleigh is our family Solicitor and he is to prepare an affidavit stating that Lady

Alphonse is still living. Why we need this, I am not at liberty to divulge, but I beg you – if the lady is here, you must tell us!"

He looked as if he felt rather uncomfortable being scrutinised by three pairs of eyes. He wriggled a little in his seat.

"We have an Amelia Alphonse in residence. She was brought in by a man claiming to be her relative. I have the paperwork here somewhere, if I can locate it."

Walking over to a bookcase filled with box files, he took one down and opened it.

The tension in the room grew as he leafed rapidly through its contents.

After a few moments, he appeared to find what he was looking for and pulled it out of the box.

"Amelia Alphonse was brought to us on the 26th of May 1849. I was not at Hanwell in those days, but my predecessor, Mr. Ellis, has written some notes here if you would care to view them."

He handed the sheaf of papers to Mr. Burleigh, who scrutinised them in silence.

"Is there a nurse or someone who would have been here at the time of the admission of Lady Alphonse?"

"Mrs. O'Brien, who brought you to my Office. She has been at Hanwell for twenty years. Would you like me to summon her?"

"If you would, Mr. Warren. I would be grateful."

Mr. Warren picked up a bell on his desk and rang it. Within seconds, a young woman appeared.

"Could you ask Mrs. O'Brien to come to my Office at once, please?"

Five minutes later, Mrs. O'Brien appeared.

"Mrs. O'Brien. Mr. Burleigh here now wishes to ask you about Amelia Alphonse – you must answer him to the best of your ability. It is very important that you try and remember anything he asks of you."

Mrs. O'Brien, looking surly, nodded.

"Mrs. O'Brien," Mr. Burleigh began, "were you here on the day Mrs. Alphonse was admitted to Hanwell."

"Yes, sir, I was."

"And she was brought in by – ?"

"A man who said 'e was 'er cousin, sir. I didn't believe 'im for a moment. I could tell 'e was 'er 'usband straight away."

"And how, may I ask, could you do this?"

"When you've been in this job as long as I 'ave, sir, you gets to recognise the signs. The 'usbands most often pretend to be someone else, a distant relative, a friend. It's *the shame*, you see, sir."

"And was this gentleman a wealthy man?"

"I thought 'e appeared so, sir. But 'e said 'e was of slender means. Said Mrs. Alphonse 'ad no 'usband and 'ad taken to wanderin' the streets in 'er nightclothes."

"And he signed the committal forms?"

"Yes, sir. In front of me very own eyes."

"Mr. Warren, might I see these papers?"

Mr. Warren made a grunting noise that indicated that he did so unwillingly, as he handed over the papers.

"Lady Brandon, would you care to take a look at this signature – '*Ignatius Alphonse*'."

Lady Brandon's hand shook as she received it.

"Yes, that is his signature," she exclaimed.

"Would you have in your possession any document with Lord Alphonse's signature on it?"

"I do, it's a receipt for the delivery of two horses – which he has yet to pay for."

She took a folded piece of paper from her bag.

Mr. Burleigh opened it and stared at the signature on the bottom.

"One and the same," he declared with satisfaction in his voice. "Now, all that remains is to see the lady in question. Mr. Warren, would that be possible?"

"Mrs. O'Brien will take you to her cell. We have to keep her confined for the safety of the other inmates, but I am afraid that you will not be able to see her, Mr. Burleigh. It's a women-only ward and you are not a relative. Some of the women are not presentable, you understand."

"Quite," answered Mr. Burleigh. "Lady Brandon, will you and your daughter go?"

"Will *you* go, Temia?" she asked. "I don't believe my nerves would permit me to see the poor wretch."

"Of course, Mama."

Mrs. O'Brien stood with an impatient look on her face. She tapped the keys on her belt and Temia rose from her chair immediately.

"Come with me, Miss Brandon."

Mrs. O'Brien led Temia out of the Office and down some more corridors. The low moaning that she had heard earlier now sounded nearer.

"I hope you're not easily shocked, miss," said Mrs. O'Brien, with obvious relish. "Amelia is not a pretty sight. She tears whatever clothes we give her and will not wash or comb her hair."

"I don't mind," answered Temia, screwing up her courage. She looked straight ahead and tried not to stare at the pathetic figures they passed.

"She gives 'erself right airs and graces, that one," added Mrs. O'Brien. "Makes us call 'er 'my Lady'!"

"She is a Lady. Her husband is a Lord."

"I 'ad guessed as much that 'e be a toff!"

Temia felt her blood boiling. Lord Alphonse had enriched himself by cheating her father! How dare he? The last time she saw him he was wearing an expensive suit of clothes and fine kid leather shoes.

At last they came to a corridor full of doors with grills. A nurse sat at the end on a wooden chair.

"Mabel, this 'ere lady wants to see Amelia. And 'ow 'as she been today?"

"In a right rage!" answered Mabel. "Bit me when I takes in 'er breakfast, 'cos I didn't call 'er 'my Lady'."

"She is often so?" asked Temia, feeling faint.

Now she was by the cell, she was not certain that she wished to see what it contained.

"More often than not, so we lock 'er up."

Mabel put the key in the lock and turned it.

"You stay behind me, miss. She can be real violent around strangers – especially ladies."

As the door opened, a dreadful smell hit Temia's nostrils. It was acrid and took her breath away.

"Come along on now, my Lady, there be someone 'ere wants to see you," coaxed Mabel.

Temia stepped inside the cell and Mrs. O'Brien at once closed the door behind them and stood guard by it.

Slowly, Temia's eyes became accustomed to the dim light. What she had taken for a bundle of rags in the corner slowly unfurled itself.

Temia saw wild staring eyes, two pools of blue in yellowing whites and straggling hair that must have once been pretty.

Lady Alphonse's claw-like hands plucked at her dirty rags.

"Where is my husband? He will want his dinner and I have not spoken to cook!" she howled.

Without a warning, she suddenly shot forward and threw herself at Mabel, her hands grasping at her skirts.

"Let me out! Let me out of here! My husband will kill you all in your beds if you don't let me out!"

Temia drew back and stepped on Mrs. O'Brien.

"See, she's as mad as a March hare!"

Lady Alphonse cocked her head to one side like a bird and then began to cry softly.

"Ignatius. Ignatius." she moaned.

Temia could not stand to see the woman any longer and she turned to Mrs. O'Brien indicating that she wished to leave. The stench was making her retch and she was overcome with pity for poor Lady Alphonse.

She felt unsteady on her feet as Mabel and Mrs. O'Brien quickly left the cell too and locked the door.

Even though the air outside was hardly any sweeter, Temia took in great gulps, as if she had been suffocated.

"Do you wish to sit down for a while, miss?" asked Mrs. O'Brien. "Them that ain't used to it feel queer after seein' an inmate."

"To sink to such depths!" murmured Temia. "It is beyond belief!"

She hesitated and then began to make her way back to Mr. Warren's Office. It was only sheer force of will that carried her forwards.

As she rejoined her mother and Mr. Burleigh, she was still shaking.

"Temia!" cried Lady Brandon. "Darling, you look so pale! Do you need smelling salts?"

"No, Mama, but I must sit down for a while."

"You saw Lady Alphonse?" asked Mr. Burleigh.

"Yes, I did. The poor soul!" whispered Temia.

"Very well, we shall take our leave, then, if you feel well enough – "

"Just a moment," answered Temia, dabbing at her face with her handkerchief.

"I am sorry you found it so distressing," continued Mr. Burleigh. "But it is necessary for us to establish Lady Alphonse's existence. Mr. Warren, I shall require a copy of Lady Alphonse's admission notes if such a thing exists."

"Naturally. We always ask whoever commits the inmate to sign in triplicate. Do you wish to examine the doctor's note as well?"

"Yes, that would be useful. They will be returned as soon as the matter is concluded. Thank you for your time, Mr. Warren. Good day."

Mr. Burleigh rose from his chair and helped Lady Brandon from hers.

Feeling a little steadier, Temia followed them out to the carriage.

She could not wait to leave those terrible corridors behind with all their hidden secrets.

Lady Brandon held onto Temia's hand tightly as the horses pulled forward while Mr. Burleigh scrutinised the documents.

They were almost back when he finally spoke,

"Lady Brandon, I think this is enough to send Lord Alphonse away for a long time. With the Duke's evidence, and your husband's, a case can be easily brought against Lord Alphonse. I will draft out the affidavit at once and contact you the moment it has been drawn up. Where will you be staying, Lady Brandon?"

"I return to Northamptonshire tomorrow morning. I have been away for long enough – my place now is at my husband's side. I have done what I came to London for."

"Very good. I will write and make an appointment for you both to visit me in my Office. I will also contact the Duke and inform him of our discovery. I am sure that he will wish to correspond with you on the matter. May I give him your address?"

"I will ask my husband first, if you don't mind. He may be angry that I have gone behind his back and I will need to discuss it all with him."

Mr. Burleigh nodded and returned to his reading.

Eventually the carriage drew up at Mrs. Timms's house. Temia felt tearful as she knew that she would now be bidding her Mama farewell.

"Darling, do write to me. Once I have explained to your father what has occurred, I am certain he will wish to welcome you back to Bovendon Hall."

"I long to see him, Mama, but the theatre – they need me and I cannot leave them. It's our opening week and Leo Baker relies upon me."

"Then we shall come to London soon and visit you, now kiss me, my dearest child."

Her eyes were full of tears as she clasped Temia.

"I have not forgotten about Sophia," she whispered, as Temia began to cry. "I promise I shall do my utmost to speak with your Papa about her and if there is any possible way that a reunion can come to pass, I shall engineer it."

"Thank you, Mama! Thank you!"

She kissed her Mama's cheek and alighted from the carriage.

*

Temia did not hurry to the theatre that evening. It was almost curtain up when she arrived backstage.

"Where have you been? Mr. Baker is going mad!" cried Sophia on seeing her wan face.

"You have forgotten that I was out with Mama this afternoon?" answered Temia, shooting her a look full of hidden meaning.

"And did you find what you were looking for?"

"We shall speak of this later," answered Temia.

"'E was 'ere again earlier," piped up Lily.

"Who are you talking about?" asked Temia stiffly.

"'Im. You know – that Earl of Wentworth!"

Temia's stomach lurched as she tried to hide her face in the skirts of the dress she had just retrieved.

"'E was standin' outside in the rain when I comes in and asks me where you was. I said you was ill. Well, I didn't know you was comin' in today, did I?"

"Did – did he say anything?"

"No, 'e just turned around and went – just like that, 'e never says much. I don't think 'e cares for me!"

"Is he in the theatre now, Lily?"

"How should I know? Most likely – "

Temia felt sick.

What would happen if Sir Thomas attended the performance that evening as well? It had been some nights since he had last visited the theatre and Temia knew that sooner or later he would appear.

In spite of herself, she found the prospect of seeing Sir Thomas not unappealing. She enjoyed his company a great deal. It was simply that she was not in love with him. But if she saw him, would he propose again?

'I don't think I have the heart to refuse him,' she thought, as the girls rushed off to the stage, 'yet, I don't have it in my heart to love him and marry him either.'

She was still pondering her dilemma when Hobson knocked on the door.

"Flowers for you, Temia!"

"Who left them?" she asked him.

"Sir Thomas Babbington," answered Hobson, "he left them at the stage door not five minutes ago."

Temia took the flowers and read the card.

"*Say you'll have supper with me, I will be waiting.*"

"Hobson," she called him back. "please don't admit anyone for me backstage tonight. I believe you know who I am referring to?"

"Them toffs?"

"Yes, if you would."

"I'll do me best!"

During the interval, Hobson returned once more to the dressing room carrying a small box.

"For you," he smirked.

"The Earl?" she asked, with her voice shaking.

"The very same."

Temia opened the box and found inside a beautiful pink orchid along with a note.

"*Meet me after the show,*" was all it said.

She felt sick with nerves by the time that the show reached its conclusion. If both of them were waiting for her, she was sure that an argument would ensue.

Could she prevent it?

"I can see your admirers are out in force tonight," commented Sophia, as she changed into her street clothes.

119

"Yes, and I don't know which way to turn. They have both asked me to dine with them and sent flowers!"

"Lord, that will cause a row! What will you do?"

"I shall remain here until they have gone and I have told Hobson not to let them in under any circumstances."

"Very well, I will wait with you," smiled Sophia.

They sat side-by-side for half an hour and then, Temia stood up.

"I cannot stay here all evening!" she groaned.

"Then, you will have to go out and face them both. I expect they'll still be here!"

Temia was not looking forward to confronting the two of them, but she knew that Sophia was right.

Picking up her cloak, she put on her hat and then her gloves as slowly as possible.

Finally, she was ready.

"I will leave these lovely flowers – "

"Come, take my hand," urged Sophia.

Temia took a deep breath and the two girls left the dressing room.

As soon as they reached the corridor that led out of the theatre, Temia could hear raised voices outside.

"Oh! Oh!" she sighed, stopping by the stage door.

"I'm sorry, I didn't think I should interfere," said Hobson with a worried look. "They've been arguing like the blazes for the last ten minutes."

Sophia squeezed Temia's hand and then turned the handle on the stage door.

As it opened, Temia could see that both men were standing tensely facing each other. Their lips were curled in anger and the Earl resembled a coiled spring.

"Repeat what you just said!" he screamed with his face just inches away from Sir Thomas's.

"I said, you are not the man you once were."

Neither men had heard the stage door open and they continued to hurl insults at each other.

Temia winced at the ferocity of their words.

She wanted to cry out and fling herself between them, but the pressure of Sophia's arm restrained her.

"Take that back!" snarled the Earl, "you snivelling excuse for a man!"

"How dare you call me that!" snapped Sir Thomas. "Look at yourself. Just what have you become? The old Wentworth would never stoop to stealing his best friend's sweetheart!"

The Earl's eyes flashed with rage. It was as if a hot mist was clouding his judgement. Tearing one of his white gloves from his waistcoat pocket, he hit Sir Thomas full in the face with it.

"There is only one way to settle this, Babbington!" he snarled, in a voice that made Temia's blood freeze, "and that is the old-fashioned way – and to the death! May the best man win!"

"No! No!" cried Temia, as the Earl strode off to his waiting carriage. "*You must not*! You must not!"

"Temia!"

Sir Thomas's face was smarting from the blow and a livid red mark was appearing on his cheek.

Seeing the Earl climb into his carriage, Temia's instinct was to run after him, but she was now frightened of him. She had never seen him so angry and did not wish him to turn on her.

"Temia, go home!" urged Sir Thomas in a tone like ice. His eyes glittered and his breath came in short bursts.

"But Thomas – "

"This is men's business. I tell you again, go home. Sophia, take her from this place. I have a matter of honour to settle before I can claim you for my own."

"Thomas, please don't fight a duel with the Earl – he is your friend."

"*Was*. Now go. Sophia, you take Temia away at once! I shall send word as soon as all this is concluded."

His harsh tone shocked her. Sophia nodded mutely and led a weeping Temia away.

"They'll not duel," she said calmly, as they walked quickly to their lodgings. "Two important gentlemen like that. They would not break the law. I'll wager that as soon as they reach the Park, they will come to their senses and shake hands."

"No, they will not," answered Temia, as they let themselves in. "I have never seen Thomas lose his temper as he did this evening and the things they screamed at each other – "

Sophia knocked on Mrs. Timms's door and asked if she might have a nip of brandy to give to Temia.

"She has had a terrible shock," she explained, as the landlady brought out a bottle and poured out a small glass.

The two girls sat up waiting for hours.

Temia stopped crying and instead remained mute and numb. The clock on the mantelpiece showed half-past two and still there was no word.

Temia had intended to tell Sophia that her mother had agreed to her meeting their father, but she could not form the words.

Although important, her thoughts were consumed with the Earl.

Would he be killed or would he kill Thomas?

Would the Police arrest them – perhaps they were already locked up in jail!

How she loved him!

A thousand thoughts whirled through her mind and she felt quite dizzy from them.

She was just nodding off when there came a loud rapping on the front door.

Both Sophia and Temia jumped and then froze.

"The messenger," whispered Sophia.

Temia was unable to speak. She held the coverlet of the bed in her hands and waited for the knock on their own door that would inevitably follow.

They heard the sound of Mrs. Timms speaking in a low voice and then her heavy footsteps on the stairs.

Clinging to each other, they waited for the knock. When it came, Sophia leapt up to answer it.

"There is a messenger here for Miss Morris."

With beating heart, Temia rose from the bed and, taking up her candle, walked towards the door.

"Shall I come with you?" asked Sophia.

"No, wait here."

As she walked down the stairs, she could not help but tremble. Standing in the door she could see the slight figure of the messenger.

But was it the Earl or Sir Thomas who sent him?

She approached the messenger at the door.

Seeing her come towards him, he tipped his hat.

"Miss Morris?" he said, stepping forward.

CHAPTER NINE

"Miss Morris?" asked the messenger again.

Temia wondered again who had sent him.

"Yes," she answered, her mouth dry and the word almost shrivelling on her lips.

"I have been sent by the Earl of Wentworth, miss. He says to tell you that it went ill for the other party and that he does not wish to see anybody. He said you would understand the message."

Temia felt her head spinning and a swoon coming over her. She clutched at the door and tried to compose herself as best she could.

"Was there any more to the message?" she asked, pulling the shawl around her tighter.

"I'm afraid not, miss."

"Thank you," she replied and closed the door.

A low wail emerged from her mouth.

She felt overcome with guilt and grief – it was all her fault! If she had told Sir Thomas that she did not love him and that her heart belonged to another, then this would not have happened.

Mrs. Timms, disturbed by the noise, came from her room to find Temia, crouched on the floor sobbing.

"Miss Temia!" she cried, putting her arm around her. "Whatever can the matter be?"

At the same moment, Sophia came hurrying down the stairs towards them.

"Temia. Temia! What is the news?"

"Poor thing, she has had a shock. Just look at her!" exclaimed Mrs. Timms, "do you know what the messenger might have said? We'll take her into my parlour. Come along, Temia. I shall make you some hot milk."

She and Sophia helped Temia her into the parlour. Mrs. Timms lit two candles and while Sophia was making Temia comfortable on the sofa, she opened a glass-fronted cabinet and produced a bottle of brandy.

"Now, you wait here, Miss Sophia, while I run to the kitchen to heat up some milk."

As soon as she had gone, Sophia knelt by Temia.

"What has happened?" she asked her in a whisper. "Was anyone hurt?"

"*Sir Thomas*! The boy did not know any more than that. He was the Earl's messenger."

Sophia gave a sharp intake of breath and then said,

"Poor Sir Thomas. Is he – ?"

"I cannot be sure, but if he was, I would imagine that the message would have been worded in such a way as to leave me in no doubt. Oh, Sophia – *it's all my fault*!"

"You must not think that, dearest."

"Then, whose is it?"

"Temia, you did not ask them to fight over you, let alone engage in a duel. That Earl's temper is so quick!"

"But Thomas did not attempt to stop the argument. His is the voice of reason when the Earl loses his temper."

"But he loves you dearly, Temia, and did not want to lose you. Were not his last words to you that he would come and claim you for his own?"

Temia dried her eyes and looked miserably into the middle distance.

"Yet I am ashamed to say that I am glad it was not the Earl who fell – "

"You love him?"

"Yes, I do. With all my heart. But it is I who has caused this terrible accident. As surely as if I had pulled the trigger myself."

Mrs. Timms came back holding a glass of milk.

"How are you, dear?" she asked.

"I-I shall be quite well soon – thank you."

"You must drink this, it's sweetened with sugar."

Temia took the milk and warmed her hands on the sides of the glass.

As she stared into the drink, she was trying to think what her best course of action might be.

Should she go to the Earl's house? But she did not know where it was.

Where would he take Sir Thomas? That would, she thought, depend upon the severity of his wounds.

She drank the milk and then felt heavy and sleepy. She was utterly drained from the events that evening and seeing the two friends at each other's throats like wolves.

And now, Sir Thomas was wounded and may even be dying!

After a while, Sophia took her up to bed.

Very soon, she was warm and cosy and drifting off to sleep, exhaustion numbing every inch of her body.

*

The scene at the house in Mount Row was frantic.

The Earl, his shirt open and coatless, had taken the wounded Sir Thomas to his house and now was loading him into a fast phaeton for the journey to Northampton.

Beside him his faithful manservant, Elliot, was busy taking orders from him.

"You are to tell no one of this, Elliot. If the Police come to the house, tell the servants to say I have gone to France on business. Under no circumstances is anyone to inform them of my whereabouts. They are to maintain that I left earlier in the evening to catch the boat to Calais."

"Yes, my Lord."

"Now, I wish you to drive us to Yardley Manor – are the horses ready?"

"They are, my Lord, I have selected only the fastest to pull the phaeton."

"And my luggage?"

"I have packed a small bag for you, my Lord. It's already on board."

"Very good, Elliot. We must leave at once. You have left word with Mrs. Murray to close up the house?"

"Yes, my Lord."

The Earl smiled. Elliot was worth his weight in gold and this was not the first time he had been asked to cover his Master's tracks."

"Excellent. And Sir Thomas, is he comfortable?"

"As much as can be expected, my Lord."

"Let's depart without further delay."

Elliot bowed and climbed up on the box.

He urged the horses on and soon, they were trotting along Park Lane.

At Marble Arch he turned the coach Northwards and out of London. With any luck they would arrive in Northampton just before daybreak.

Elliot realised it was imperative that they travel at night and he would not stop for anyone or anything. His

Master's reputation and the life of his friend both depended on his skill and the swiftness of the horses.

Inside Sir Thomas moaned as the carriage wheels rumbled over the rough road.

"Ssh," exhorted the Earl.

He cradled his injured friend and tried to staunch the bleeding underneath his coat.

The bullet had gone straight through and out of the other side. The Earl constantly relived the moment that, with his blood up, he had shot his friend.

He had aimed to kill, but had not reckoned on his pistol sight being out of alignment. He had aimed for Sir Thomas's heart and had him hit just under his ribs.

It was only when he had sunk to his knees that the Earl had been brought to his senses.

Although he had a hot temper, he could be cool under stress and did not panic. He had loaded Thomas into his carriage and had the driver take them to his house in Mount Row and then gave the man a big tip to keep quiet.

'I pray he is as discreet as Elliot, otherwise I am in deep trouble,' murmured the Earl, as they sped on.

A heavily bleeding man in a fast phaeton would only serve to arouse suspicion if they were stopped.

Some hours later, the phaeton finally rumbled up the long drive of Yardley Manor.

It was an elegant Jacobean house that the Earl's father had much improved on with two new wings.

And now, it seemed as if all his hopes of bringing Temia to the Manor as his wife were about to be dashed.

He sighed with relief as the carriage pulled up at the front entrance to Yardley Manor.

Elliot moved swiftly and woke up the hall boy, who ran to the stables to arouse the Head Groom.

"Get him inside," thundered the Earl.

Between them, they carried the semi-conscious Sir Thomas inside and into one of the guest rooms.

"Fetch Mrs. Hopkins at once and then send a stable boy to the village for Doctor Soul. Hurry, we don't have any time to lose."

"He has lost a lot of blood," commented Elliot.

"Ask Mrs. Hopkins to bring some old sheets. We shall rebind his wounds until Doctor Soul can tend to him."

Elliot left the room, as Sir Thomas suddenly came to and stared about him with wide eyes.

"Wentworth?" he murmured. "Are you there?"

In a flash the Earl was at his friend's side.

"Babbington, you have been badly wounded, you must not move. The doctor will be here soon."

"It's not like you to miss such an obvious target, Richard. You must have – lost your nerve!"

He tried to laugh, but it came out as a splutter.

"Enough, Thomas," the Earl replied gently. "You must stay calm and not move until Doctor Soul arrives."

"And Temia?"

"I have sent word to her of the outcome."

"Telling her what? That you will come and claim her as yours as soon as I have expired?"

The Earl shook his head.

"No, Thomas. I have not."

"I did not wish to fight you, Richard. This could have been avoided but, for once, I lost my temper. Ha! Did you hear that? *I* lost *my* temper!"

Just then, Elliot came into the room carrying a tray that held a bottle and two glasses.

"My Lord, I thinks some brandy would be in order – for medicinal purposes."

"Thank you, Elliot. Is Mrs. Hopkins on her way?"

"She is, my Lord. She has been told that under no circumstances must she alert any of the other servants. We don't want them talking."

"Just tell them that Babbington's pistol went off in his coat by accident – a faulty catch."

"Very good, my Lord."

The Earl looked at his wounded friend and his heart rent in two. How could he have done such a thing? His best friend since boyhood and he had shot him over *a woman*!

But Temia was not just any woman. She was the woman he adored and who he could never forget. Even when Sir Thomas had told him that he intended to propose, it had not quenched the fire within his heart. Her image was burned onto it as surely as if she had branded him.

"Here, drink this, Thomas," he urged.

"I hope it's your best!"

"Naturally."

The Earl was feeling sick with worry. His friend's face held a grey hue and his lips were pale and going blue.

It did not look good.

Mrs. Hopkins was a calm businesslike woman who went about dressing his wound with fresh bandages made from old sheets.

"Come along now, sir," she coaxed in her motherly fashion. "You're going to have to sit up a little."

Sir Thomas cried out in pain as she pulled away the bloodied pieces of cloth closest to the wound.

"Where is that damned doctor?" the Earl called out in a fraught tone. "He should be here by now."

"My Lord – he has to come from Denton and the roads are perilous."

He paced up and down worrying about Sir Thomas and Temia.

It was not the prospect of prison that concerned him or the scandal and the ruination of his good family name. No, he was far more concerned about losing his dear friend as well as his beloved Temia.

Had she not seen enough to frighten her away?

How could she ever love a man with such a violent nature? Would it not be too easy for her to conclude that if he stooped to attempting to kill the man who was supposed to be his best friend – he might strike a woman?

'I am a fool and a coward,' he thought, as he paced the room while Mrs. Hopkins finished her ministrations. 'I am *not* a man! My blessed temper always sees to that.'

He struck his fist hard on the marble mantelpiece.

'I shall never forgive myself if he dies. *Never*!'

He thought of the last time he had been challenged to a duel – that night at the Club by the Frenchman. With a bitter grimace, he recalled how Thomas had saved him from harm then and had scolded him for losing his temper – saying that one day it would be his undoing.

He had not thought then that his prophesy would come true in such a tragic fashion.

"My Lord, Doctor Soul is here."

The Earl turned and saw the doctor enter.

"My Lord," he took off his hat and bowed.

"Don't stand on such ceremony, man. My friend is badly injured!"

The doctor put down his bag and went to the couch where Sir Thomas lay prostrate. He checked his pulse and pulled back the torn and bloody shirt to inspect the wound.

131

"Mrs. Hopkins has just dressed it."

"And she has tied the bindings tightly, I see. That is good. However, I shall need to take them off to examine the wound itself."

The Earl winced as he unravelled the bindings to reveal the ragged hole where the bullet had entered.

"The bullet has exited his body cleanly," remarked Doctor Soul, "but he has lost a great deal of blood. We must get him into bed at once."

"And will he live?" asked the Earl, his dark eyes as black as pitch.

"I could not say, my Lord. I have seen men survive wounds such as this, but the next twenty-fours hours will be crucial. Should he survive them, then there is every chance he will recover. I cannot tell what damage has been done to his organs and we can only hope and pray that the bullet did not pass through his liver."

"Is there no way of telling?"

"I am afraid not. We cannot see inside the patient. There is no bleeding from the mouth, which is a good sign but, other than that, it's a matter of time and prayer."

The Earl stared at his friend.

"He might die?" he asked suddenly.

"It's a possibility. He will need careful nursing."

"Then, he shall have whatever he needs, money is no object, doctor. Will you arrange a nurse for him?"

"I shall send for one immediately. There is a lady in a nearby village who is highly skilled and was trained by Miss Florence Nightingale herself. I shall engage her."

"Nothing is too good for Sir Thomas."

As the doctor turned to leave, the Earl touched his arm.

"Nothing needs to be said about this outside these four walls. Is that understood?"

The doctor, a man of the world and one who knew a pistol wound when he saw one, nodded his head.

Whatever had passed between these two gentlemen was no concern of his and he knew that the Earl would be most generous when it came to settling his bill.

"I will return tomorrow morning, my Lord. Mrs. Hopkins should keep him warm until the nurse comes and you must send for me at once if there is any change."

"Thank you very much, Doctor Soul."

As the doctor departed, Mrs. Hopkins reappeared to take away the brandy.

"Leave it!" snapped the Earl. "And close the door behind you. You are to admit no one without my say-so, is that clear?"

"Yes, my Lord," she said with a startled look.

"Now, leave us. I shall ring for you if anything is required. Please show the nurse in the minute she arrives."

Mrs. Hopkins was familiar with the Earl's temper. It sometimes frightened her.

'Them flashing eyes!' she muttered, as she closed the door. 'I wouldn't care to incur their wrath!'

The nurse arrived very early the next morning and was quickly informed that her discretion was paramount.

The Earl did not leave Sir Thomas's side – much to the consternation of his servants.

*

Over the next days, the Earl neither ate, washed, shaved nor even changed his clothes. Instead, he paced the room like a cat, drinking his way through several bottles of brandy and refusing all food.

'He'll not eat or sleep and he'll make himself ill soon and Doctor Soul will have two patients on his hands!' murmured Mrs. Hopkins, taking away a tray of untouched food.

Sir Thomas had not regained consciousness and he appeared to be sinking slowly.

He cried out in his delirium for Temia and hearing her name wrung the Earl's heart.

"Temia! Temia!" called Sir Thomas with his eyes closed and sweat on his brow.

The Earl did not care one jot what he looked like – all he cared about was the recovery of his friend.

'Temia! *Darling*!' the Earl anguished every now and then.

He missed Temia terribly and loved her more than he could say. His love for her wracked his frame and tore at his heart – it tortured him through the long nights and was still there, bright and fresh, in the morning.

He went to Sir Thomas's side and saw that he was opening his eyes.

The doctor had come that very morning and said, in confidence, that he was not getting better.

"It's as if he has just lost the will to live," he had pronounced in a sombre tone. "All my skill as a physician is useless if the patient himself does not wish to recover. And this man appears not to care if he dies."

"Wentworth!"

Sir Thomas's voice was feeble and hoarse.

"What is it, Babbington?"

"Temia. I – must – see her!"

"She is in London. You are in Northampton."

"Wentworth, I know that I am not too long for this world. If I could just kiss her dear face once more, then I could die a happy man. Just grant me this, my once-dear friend and we shall forget any bad blood between us!"

Despite himself, the Earl felt a lump rising in his throat. As he looked into his friend's pleading eyes, he knew he must try and right the wrong he had committed.

"You mean, Thomas, bring her – here?"

"Please, my friend. Do this one thing for me."

The two men looked at each other.

The Earl regarded his pale face and thought that, much as it would cause him distress – and indeed to Temia as well – he could not refuse him."

"Very well, I shall write to her."

Sir Thomas clung onto his sleeve.

"Thank you, Richard," he murmured, before falling back into unconsciousness.

*

The days had also seemed long and without hope for Temia.

She simply went through the motions of her duties at the theatre, but her heart was elsewhere. She became pale and wan, losing weight and not eating.

Sophia was terribly worried about her and did her best to encourage her.

"You must eat something," she warned, as Temia again refused the food she had brought to her.

"I cannot until I know exactly what has happened to Sir Thomas," she answered, turning her face away.

"If he has died, we would have heard. All London would be talking about it. We get enough toffs in here that someone would have said something."

"That is true, but not to know is like a slow death."

"Temia, you must forget them. Your mother and father will need you when Lord Alphonse is arrested. Did she not say she would write to you and let you know?"

"Yes, she did, but it was last week and these things don't happen overnight. Even if Mr. Burleigh has gone to the Police, it will take time. Supposing Lord Alphonse has got wind of this and has left the country?"

"What and leave rich pickings behind? From what you have said, he is not a man to be easily discouraged."

Just then, a boy put his head around the door.

"Scuse me, ladies. Miss Temia Morris?"

"I am she," answered Temia.

"Mr. Baker asked me to give this to you."

The boy handed over a letter.

Temia almost dropped it when she saw the crest.

Her hands began to shake and she clutched at her wildly beating heart.

"Temia, what is it"? asked Sophia

"It's come from the Earl," she whispered, turning the letter over in her hand. "The crest – it's his."

"You must open it!"

Temia paused and then did so.

Drawing out the sheet of fine paper, she read the contents and then sighed,

"Sir Thomas wishes to see me. Oh, Sophia, he is dying!"

"Did he write the letter?"

"No, the Earl did. He says that Sir Thomas is at death's door and is asking for me. I am to come at once."

"But then you don't know if it's safe for you to go home!" cried Sophia. "What if that Lord Alphonse sees you around in the County? He could kidnap you and, then, where would we all be? Don't forget, it is *you* who saw his wife in the asylum. You are an important witness."

"This I know, Sophia. But I cannot stay here while Sir Thomas is dying."

"And you cannot go alone," said Sophia, picking up her coat. "We will go straight to Leo Baker and ask if we can be excused from the theatre. I am coming with you."

"Oh, Sophia, would you?"

"You try stopping me!"

Leo Baker was not at all happy that two of his girls wanted to take some time off. It was only through Sophia pleading with him that a friend was dying that he relented.

"Very well, but only a few days, mind. I want you back for Saturday's performance. Full house, it is!"

"We promise. Thank you, Mr. Baker."

Within an hour the two girls had gone back to their lodgings, packed a bag each and were in a Hackney cab on their way to Euston Station.

They bought two tickets for Northampton and sat down to wait for their train.

"Where shall we stay?" asked Sophia. "We can hardly arrive at your parents' house – me the long-lost, half sister and you, the fugitive!"

"I had not thought – " answered Temia, dreamily. "But there's bound to be a hotel or inn and it cannot be any worse than Mrs. Timms!"

Sophia laughed.

"Perhaps, the Earl will allow us to stay with him."

"Oh, I could not ask such a thing!" replied Temia, shocked. "It would not be at all right. No, we shall ask at Northampton Station for somewhere suitable."

Temia had never felt so nervous in her life, as she sat on the train. Not even when she had fled to London some weeks earlier.

She so wished that she was meeting the Earl under different circumstances and was apprehensive at seeing Sir Thomas.

At Northampton the girls were fortunate enough to encounter a friendly woman and she gave them a lift to a nearby hotel that she said was suitable for young ladies.

The hotel arranged for a carriage to take Temia to Yardley Manor and, by nightfall, she was on her way.

Sophia remained at the hotel to wait for her, as she had not thought it right to intrude.

Temia felt guilty for leaving her behind, but she knew she had no choice. She tried not to dwell upon how Sir Thomas would be, instead she thought of home.

'So near and yet so far!' she said to herself, trying to see the Northamptonshire countryside in the pitch-black outside the carriage window.

Yardley Manor was only a few miles away from Bovendon Hall and it was surely a miracle that she had never met the Earl before.

'Of course, had he attended the ball that my parents had thrown for me on my return from Paris, things might have turned out differently,' she reflected, as the carriage made its way up the long drive of Yardley Manor.

As they pulled up at the front door, she saw the Earl rush towards the carriage.

She scarcely recognised the raggle-taggle figure who greeted her.

His hair was unkempt, he had the beginnings of a beard and his clothes were torn and filthy. He looked more like a field hand than an Earl.

"*Temia!*"

Opening the carriage door, he did not give her any time to set foot on the drive as he swept her up in his arms and held her close.

"Temia, darling! I am so glad to see you!" he cried, covering her face in kisses.

His beard prickled, but she did not care.

When he then pressed his mouth to hers, she did not resist. She melted into his embrace and gave herself up into a long passionate kiss.

She felt that they were both touching Heaven for a moment of blinding ecstasy.

"How can you ever forgive me for what I did?" he murmured, stroking her face tenderly. "I behaved really reprehensibly."

"I could forgive you anything because I love you," she replied, looking at him with blue eyes full of emotion.

"*You love me*? After all that I did?" he gasped, incredulously. "Temia, I love you deeply, but I did not dare to hope – "

"Then, hush. This is no time for recriminations."

"I love you so much!" he cried, kissing her again.

Temia trembled as his strong arms crushed her. She could feel his heart beating against her and longed to stay like this forever.

"Thomas – I should go to him," she said, pulling herself away from his embrace.

"Yes, of course."

The Earl's face was flushed and his eyes were great pools of darkness.

He escorted her to the room where Sir Thomas lay.

The nurse sat beside him, reading by the light of an oil lamp and Temia thought she looked very kind.

"How is he?" asked the Earl, as they entered.

"Temia? Is that you?"

Sir Thomas pulled himself up from his pillows, his face white and shining with sweat.

"I am here, Thomas," she answered softly, before turning to the nurse and saying, "may I speak with you?"

She rose and walked out into the corridor.

"What is his condition?" asked Temia.

"Very sick. He seems to have no will to live. He will not eat. If only he would take some nourishment, then he would have a chance."

"Then I will stay with him until he eats something," said Temia, decisively. "You must be tired. I am certain you would like some rest. Please leave me with him and I will send for you if he deteriorates."

The nurse smiled and left her.

Temia opened the door and returned to the bedside.

"Temia, you have come! I knew you would."

Sir Thomas stretched out a hand and took hers. He looked so ill that she wanted to cry.

"Richard, have your cook send some hot beef tea at once and then leave us, please."

"But, Temia, you have only just arrived and I have hardly had the opportunity to speak to you."

"Leave us!" she commanded, in a firm voice. "And I suggest you might like to make yourself presentable."

With reluctance and not a little embarrassment, the Earl withdrew.

As he turned at the door, he saw Temia take off her coat and bonnet and sink down in the chair by the bed.

"Thomas – " he heard her say, as he closed the door behind him.

CHAPTER TEN

The Earl paced impatiently up and down outside the room. He could hear the low murmur of voices inside, but could not decipher what was being said.

Mrs. Hopkins came along presently with some beef tea and she was admitted to the room.

As she left, she gave the Earl a long hard stare.

"Miss Temia asks if you have washed and changed yet. Am I to tell her, next time I return, that you have not yet done so?"

The Earl's fine features reddened. And now he felt ashamed of himself.

"Mrs. Hopkins, will you have Elliot draw me a bath at once, please?" he murmured, not meeting her eye.

"At once, my Lord," she answered with a satisfied look on her face.

He did not worry about Mrs. Hopkins's opinion of him, but what Temia thought was of great concern to him.

He took one last look at the closed door and then moved away. As he walked along the corridor to his room, he caught sight of himself in the large ornate mirror that hung near the staircase.

With mounting horror, he saw his bearded face and scruffy torn clothing.

'Is this how I greeted Temia?' he said to himself. 'Looking as if I have been sleeping in a haystack and then struck by a threshing machine!'

He shook his head and wondered what had become of him. What Babbington had said to him, about how he had lost his way since his father had died, was true!

'My father would not wish me to behave as I have,' he said to himself. 'He set great store by good manners and fine breeding. I have shown neither of late and to think I ignored Babbington's well-meaning lectures! It should be me, laying there dying of a pistol wound and not him!'

He shook his head again and went up to his room.

As he entered, Elliot was supervising three maids, who were bringing cans of hot water to his dressing room. A large bathtub was in the corner and they were filling it.

"My Lord, shall I dispose of those clothes you are wearing? There's your dressing gown warming by the fire and you can change into it until your bath be ready."

He went to the fire, picked up the dressing gown and then went behind the screen.

He did not feel any self-consciousness as he peeled off his filthy clothes. He felt as if he was shedding an old dead skin like a snake and that he was about to be reborn.

Elliot announced that the bath was ready and the Earl stepped out from behind the screen. Slipping into the deliciously hot water, he felt the tension flood out of him.

Elliot was standing by, ready to employ a cut-throat razor at the Earl's command.

He soaped his aching body and thought of Temia.

What was she saying to Thomas?

Would she re-emerge from the room with the news that she was going to marry him – out of pity?

Was she bargaining with him –

'Drink the beef tea and I will marry you?'

By the time he summoned Elliot to come and attend to his shaving, he was feeling desperate.

'I love her so much!' he told himself, as the razor was deftly whisked over his face. 'I don't think I could bear to lose her now.'

Later, as Elliot helped dress him, he began to feel more like his old self again. He was not a man to give up easily and neither would he in the battle for Temia's hand.

Had she not told him that she loved him?

He walked slowly downstairs to dine alone.

Mrs. Hopkins gave an approving look as she passed him and he smiled to himself as he sat down and waited for dinner to be served.

"Is there any sign of Miss Morris?" he asked, as the butler served him.

"Miss Morris, my Lord?"

"Yes, the lady who is sitting with Sir Thomas."

"Her name is Miss Brandon, my Lord, and not Miss Morris. She is the only daughter of Sir Arthur Brandon of Bovendon Hall. His horses are justly famous throughout the County for being the best in Northamptonshire, if not in England."

"*Really*?" answered the Earl, taken aback.

Even though Sir Thomas had mentioned in passing that Temia had told him she was fleeing from an arranged marriage, he had no idea her family were so well bred.

"Sir Arthur – is he in residence at the moment?

"I believe so, my Lord. He is a country gentleman and does not own a London residence."

He mulled over this information as he chewed on his lamb chops. Had not Thomas also told him her father was being blackmailed?

He resolved to make discreet enquiries as soon as the present emergency was over.

The fact that Temia had not chosen to confide in him was of no consequence to him and it certainly did not make him love her any less. In fact, he thought it showed a remarkable strength of character and he did not care for silly females who cried for attention at the slightest excuse. He far preferred women with spirit and determination.

'Yes, I shall explore this further,' he decided.

His thoughts were interrupted by Elliot.

"My Lord, Miss Temia has sent me to you. It's Sir Thomas."

"He is not – "

"No, my Lord. Quite the opposite. She has sent word that he has taken some nourishment and requests that the doctor be summoned first thing in the morning."

"Thank Heaven! Will Miss Temia be joining me for dinner?"

"No, my Lord. She has requested that no one enter the room apart from servants bringing whatever she might require. Sir Thomas is still not out of the woods."

*

In spite of being exhausted, the Earl could not sleep and he tossed and turned, half-dreaming, half-awake.

He longed to see Temia and to cover her face with kisses and tell her how much she meant to him.

At five o'clock in the morning, he arose from his large four-poster bed and paced the room. At six he rang for Elliot to bring hot coffee and boiled eggs.

By seven o'clock he was washed and dressed.

He decided to go for a ride to help ease the tension, and before he made for the stables, he went to the West wing to see if there were any signs of life.

As he passed the room where Sir Thomas lay, an exhausted Temia half-fell out of the door.

He caught her in his arms as she swooned.

"Richard!"

"Temia – are you all right?" he asked anxiously.

"I am – very tired. Is the doctor on his way?"

"Yes, is Babbington deteriorating?"

"No, Richard. He has awakened and asked for eggs and coffee!"

"Darling! My poor dear, brave darling!" he sighed, holding her closer to him.

"Excuse me, my Lord, Doctor Soul is here. Shall I show him in?"

The butler was standing there waiting expectantly.

"Show him in at once!"

"I hope that he confirms my prognosis that Thomas has turned a corner," whispered Temia in a voice that was hoarse with exhaustion.

Doctor Soul was quick to examine the patient and then to convey the good news.

"He will live and it is all thanks to this remarkable young lady. I see that he has eaten something at last."

"Yes, he had two small cups of beef tea last night and then two eggs this morning," Temia replied proudly.

"And now, young lady, I suggest that *you* rest."

Temia was taken to a guest room and brought some breakfast. The Earl gave his staff orders that she was not to be disturbed.

Several hours later, just as it was getting dark again, Temia awoke to find herself in a strange bed.

For a moment she could not remember where she was and then she realised.

'I am at Yardley Manor and Thomas is better!'

She rang for a maid and asked her to bring some hot water and then noticed a clean dress hung on a hook.

"Whose is that?" she asked the maid.

"His Lordship said to leave it out for you, miss. It used to belong to his sister."

Temia bathed and then put on the dress. It fitted her to perfection.

She did her hair and thought how once she could not have done so, but working at the theatre had made her very self-sufficient and independent.

Once presentable, she hurried to Sir Thomas, eager to discover his progress.

But the faithful Elliot barred the way.

"I am sorry, miss, but his Lordship has given strict instructions that they are not to be disturbed. He said to give you this when you awoke."

Temia opened it and read,

"My darling,

There are things that Babbington and I must thrash out, man to man. I will send for you when all is well. A carriage has been made ready to take you wherever you desire. Just know I love you very much whatever happens.

Your own Richard."

'He is sending me away!' she thought. 'Did he not mean what he said yesterday, after all?'

With a heavy heart, she gathered up the few things she had with her and went out to the waiting carriage.

She knew that she could not go home to Bovendon Hall and so she asked the driver to take her to the hotel where Sophia would be waiting for news.

"I was so worried!" she cried, as Temia reappeared. "I didn't know what to think when you didn't return. I told

146

the manager that we wanted the room for another day at least – are we staying?"

"I don't know," she answered, looking dazed.

"Temia. What's happened. How is Sir Thomas?"

"I sat up with him all night and he is recovering."

"And now?"

"The Earl has sent me away and said he will come and fetch me later."

"You must not concern yourself. Men must be left to themselves and we should not interfere with them. Have you thought more of returning home to your parents?"

"How can I? Timing is now crucial. If I was to appear before my mother has had word from Mr. Burleigh that the affidavit has been drawn up to have Lord Alphonse arrested, it would spell disaster. No, we must wait here. I will write to Mama and tell her where I am."

Temia began to write and after finishing the letter, Sophia took it to the concierge to be delivered at once.

"You should go back to bed, Temia. Look – you can scarcely keep your eyes open. Tomorrow, we'll talk. I have some news for you!"

"What is it, dearest?"

"No," smiled Sophia, mysteriously. "It can wait, but it is nothing to concern yourself with."

Temia watched as Sophia almost skipped out of the room.

'I wonder what ails her?' she said to herself, taking off her slippers.

Sophia did not return to her room until quite late, but Temia was fast asleep by then.

*

They both slept soundly and were awakened by the waiter with their breakfast.

147

Sophia eagerly tucked into toast and kedgeree.

"I love it," she exclaimed.

Temia laughed.

"I am pleased you are so happy, now what is the news you wish to tell me, Sophia?"

"I've met a gentleman!" she cried with a brilliant smile. "At a piano recital in the hotel. Oh, Temia! He is so handsome and dashing! He's a Captain and is stationed at Weedon Barracks. He saw that I was alone and asked if I needed a chaperone!"

"Sophia! That is quite shocking!"

"Oh, don't concern yourself, Temia. He is quite the gentleman. I dined with him last night and I am seeing him again this evening! So, if we stay here for a month, I could not be happier!"

"Then, I am so pleased for you, dearest," replied Temia, laying a hand fondly on her shoulder.

They were disturbed by a knocking on the door.

"That waiter is efficient – we have scarcely finished our breakfast," said Temia, as Sophia rushed to open it.

Lady Brandon swept into the room.

"You must be Sophia," she smiled. "I should have known you at once as your eyes are just like Arthur's."

Sophia blushed and dropped a curtsy.

"My Lady!" she said with her head bowed.

"Now, now – what is this nonsense? You must not kowtow to me!"

"Mama! You have received my letter?"

"Yes, darling. And I have come to tell you that you must come to The Hall at once. Yesterday afternoon we received word from Mr. Burleigh that he is to arrive at The Hall the very same evening and then, as if by a miracle, a letter arrived from Lord Alphonse announcing that he was coming to call in his debt the next day."

"He is coming to The Hall this afternoon?"

"Yes. In his letter, he said that he would be coming to take away more horses, as the bargain we made was left unfulfilled. Mr. Burleigh is delighted at the timing and is meeting with the Chief Constable. He is arranging a little reception committee!"

"Mama, this is wonderful news."

"And we shall naturally need you at The Hall. You are the lure to set the trap, Temia!"

"But Papa – he has agreed to this?"

"Darling, he is full of remorse with how he behaved towards you. He cannot wait to see you."

"And Sophia?"

"I have told him of her existence, but we must take this one step at a time. It was quite a shock for him, as you can imagine. Now, make haste. I have the carriage outside and we must return to The Hall at once. Sophia, you don't mind waiting here, do you?"

Sophia smiled shyly and bowed her head. She was so delighted that she did not wish to show her eagerness.

"Perhaps that handsome Captain of yours will take you for a drive," suggested Temia.

"I think I should stay behind in case the Earl comes for you. After all, we don't want him thinking you have run off again, do we?"

Temia thought how wise she was and she had not considered that eventuality.

"Very well. But don't stay a prisoner in your room. I am certain that your Captain would enjoy some tea in the restaurant should he come to see you!"

Sophia blushed and giggled.

Temia felt so happy to see the old family carriage outside the hotel that she almost wept.

"How is Papa?" asked Temia, as they set off.

"Very eager to see you, my dearest. When I told him what we discovered in Hanwell, he was delighted. But first, we need you to help trap Lord Alphonse. You will, won't you, after how shabbily you have been treated?"

Temia's eyes filled with tears.

"Of course, Mama! You must not think that I have stopped loving you both because of what happened. I will help in any way I can."

"I think it best to wait until Lord Alphonse is fully removed from the scene before we should introduce your father to Sophia, however."

"I agree, Mama. We have plenty of time to do so. Sophia will not mind. She has waited all these years and a few more days will not make any difference!"

By the time they reached Bovendon Hall, Temia was feeling nervous at the prospect of seeing her father again after all that had happened.

But she need not have worried. As soon as he saw her, he took her into his arms and held her fast.

"Darling! Can you forgive me for being so weak?" he said with a tremor of emotion in his voice.

"Papa, you must not even think of it. We have an important task ahead. Is Mr. Burleigh here yet?"

"He is now in the library with two Police Officers who have just arrived. He will outline the plan of action when you see him. You must be brave, Temia."

"Don't worry. I fear nothing from Lord Alphonse!"

Mr. Burleigh shook her hand warmly as she entered the library. The two Police Officers jumped to their feet as he introduced them.

"This is the Chief Constable and Sergeant Mills. They will hide in the room next to the library when Lord Alphonse arrives," he explained. "We shall leave the door ajar and, once he has incriminated himself – as he will surely do – we will jump out and present him, first with the affidavit and then these two Officers will arrest him."

"And the Duke?"

"He wanted to come, but I persuaded him that he would not be required. Between ourselves, His Grace has a filthy temper and I do not trust him not to lash out."

"Quite, we don't wish for our case to be diminished by a hot-tempered Duke!" remarked Lady Brandon. "Now, shall I ring for tea? We have something of a wait until the appointed hour arrives."

*

Lord Alphonse was very punctual. As the clock in the hall struck half-past three, Ridley came into the library and announced his arrival.

"Everyone to their places!" urged Lady Brandon.

As she passed Temia, she squeezed her hand.

"Be brave, darling," she whispered.

Temia took her place in the next room.

The plan was that she was to come in a little after Lord Alphonse. Mr. Burleigh popped his head around the door and smiled.

Lord Alphonse then swaggered into the room as if he owned it. Without waiting to be asked, he sat down on a comfortable chair and looked at Sir Arthur expectantly.

"Well? Are the horses ready for me?"

"No, they are not," answered Sir Arthur quietly.

"Then you leave me no alternative," he snarled with a self-satisfied smile. "Either you give me the two horses I requested or, when I leave here, I will pay a call upon my friend who works for the *Westminster Review*. I am certain that he will be interested to hear how one of the respected gentlemen of the County has an illegitimate daughter by a common dancer!"

Sir Arthur paused, as if considering.

"I refuse," he declared firmly.

"So, not only do you not honour your bargain, but, also, you now deny me what is mine?"

"They are not *yours*. They belong to this family!"

Just then Temia entered the room.

Lord Alphonse's expression changed from one of anger to amusement.

"Well, well, what do have we here? The runaway bride herself! This time, madam, you will not escape me!"

He rose from his chair in a flash and grabbed Temia by the arm. Twisting the tender flesh, he brought his face level with hers.

"And this time, my very fine lady, you will not run away! I shall make certain of it. Sir Arthur, your daughter has unwittingly provided you with a reprieve. Of course, I shall require compensation for your refusal to give me the horses, but no matter, I shall return once I have made this woman my wife."

"Let go, you are hurting me!" cried Temia, hoping that the Police Officers would not stay in the next room for much longer.

"And I will hurt you even more if you try to escape! I can see you need a firm hand. I shall not be sparing the rod with you, Temia!"

An evil smile spread across his face as Temia stared into his cold eyes and shuddered.

Just as he was about to drag her from the room, Mr. Burleigh rushed in with the Police Officers.

"Hold on one moment, Lord Alphonse!"

Taking the affidavit from his pocket, he brandished it at the astonished Lord.

"You are in no position to marry again with a wife still very much alive!"

Lord Alphonse looked so shocked that he almost let go of Temia.

"What is this nonsense?" he sneered with a defiant curl of his lip. "My wife is dead – everyone knows that."

"She lives still," answered Mr. Burleigh, "and this affidavit is proof. Chief Constable, Lord Alphonse's wife is an inmate of Hanwell asylum. Arrest him!"

The two Police Officers sprang forward and caught hold of Lord Alphonse.

Temia wrenched herself free from his grip and ran to her father's side.

"Lord Alphonse, I am arresting you on suspicion of attempted blackmail, extortion and bigamy on two counts," intoned the Chief Constable with relish.

"Preposterous! Unhand me!"

But the Sergeant had already clamped the handcuffs around his wrists and was busy locking them.

"Let me go!" shouted Lord Alphonse. "I will sue for wrongful arrest! What occurs in this room is a private matter. It's Sir Arthur you should be arresting for agreeing to my marrying his daughter and, then, encouraging her to run away! I am the injured party here and not him!"

"And His Grace, the Duke of Weybridge? Do you deny that two weeks ago you went to him and attempted the very same blackmail and demanded, in return for your silence, the hand of his sister?"

Lord Alphonse turned pale.

He hung his head and refused to look at either Mr. Burleigh or the Chief Constable.

"Mr. Burleigh here is his Solicitor and His Grace brought the matter to his attention. Now, if you will come with me, my Lord."

"Whore!" spat Lord Alphonse at Temia, as he was forcibly taken from the room.

"He is no gentleman!" commented Mr. Burleigh, shaking his head. "My dear, are you all right?"

Temia felt a little shaken by the vitriolic way Lord Alphonse had cursed her.

"I am all right, thank you. If all he has are spiteful words, then, as you say, he is not a gentleman."

Sir Arthur beamed and put his arm around her.

"It is all thanks to you that this awful matter has been concluded. How can I ever thank you, Temia?"

"There is one thing, I would ask, Papa. It concerns Sophia."

Sir Arthur looked a little shaken, but he nodded his head in agreement.

"What would you ask of me?"

"She is all alone in the world. Could she not come and live here with us? That is, if Mama will allow it."

"Two daughters! Although no one can ever replace Jasper in my heart, another daughter I would welcome with open arms. This house is far too empty!"

Sir Arthur sat down and thought for a moment. He was not a man given to impulsive action.

"Let me meet her first and then I shall decide."

"Thank you, Papa.

"Excuse me, miss, but there's a driver outside who says that the Earl of Wentworth has sent him. He requests that you come at once."

Ridley stood there waiting for her reply.

"Go to him, darling," urged her Mama. "I shall take the carriage to your hotel and bring Sophia back to The Hall. That is with your permission, Arthur."

"Of course, I would like to meet her and the sooner, the better!"

Temia smiled as Ridley brought out her bonnet and coat and her heart was beating wildly as she climbed into the carriage.

What lay in wait for her at Yardley Manor?

An hour later she felt sick as the carriage stopped.

The Earl was waiting for her in the hall and he took her in his arms and kissed her gently.

"Come, Temia, Thomas is waiting. Don't worry, he is much better. He is sitting up in bed and has eaten a great deal at luncheon."

Temia wondered what had passed between the two men.

She gave the Earl a puzzled look.

"There are matters that still require resolution," he murmured, as he opened the door of Sir Thomas's room.

"Temia!"

He was sitting up in bed and on seeing Temia, he shooed the nurse away.

"What was it you wanted to say to me, Thomas?"

Temia sat down on the bed and he gently took her hand and looked deep into her eyes.

"Dearest Temia, you know that I love you and wish to make you my wife, but Richard has said that it is he whom you love. If this is so, I need to hear it from your own lips. Don't spare me. If you really love Richard, then I cannot stand in your way. I love you enough to want you to be happy and, if that means you marrying him and not me, then so be it. So tell me, Temia, who do you love?"

Temia felt startled.

In spite of herself, tears sprang to her eyes. She knew that the time had come to be honest with him.

"I love Richard, Thomas – I do not love you. I am very fond of you and I am deeply flattered that you asked me to marry you, but you know I cannot."

"Then, go and be happy with him. I have decided that once I am recovered, I will go on a Grand Tour. I will not attend your wedding, but you have my blessing. Now, go. Next time I see you, you will be Lady Wentworth!"

"Thomas – "

"No, don't say anything more. You are a wonderful woman, Temia. You are beautiful as you are brave. Now you have to go. Wentworth is waiting for you. Don't keep him in suspense as he loves you so very much."

Temia rose and kissed him on the cheek. She was crying so much she could hardly see his face.

Wiping away the tears, she left the room, her heart aching profoundly.

'Never did a man give up so much – in the name of friendship,' she mumbled, as she went back downstairs.

*

A servant came and asked her to go straight to the drawing room, where the Earl was standing by a blazing fire.

On seeing her, his eyes lit up and he raced to her.

"Temia!"

156

"Oh, Richard!" she cried, as he enfolded her in his strong arms.

She could feel his heartbeat beneath his waistcoat, matching her own.

He took her in his arms and kissed her tenderly.

She felt herself overwhelmed by love that seemed to spring from Heaven itself and she felt that she was about to enter the Gates of Paradise.

Breathlessly, she pulled away from him. Her eyes full of emotion.

"Richard – he has set us free! He is going away."

"I know, he told me. As soon as he is well again. There is no obstacle now. And Lord Alphonse?"

"Locked up in jail. He will not trouble me or my family again."

"Then, my darling, are you free to marry me as soon as possible? Say you that will, Temia. I love you so much and cannot wait another minute for us to be together as one for ever. Man and wife!"

Temia thought that she had touched Heaven as she saw the love in his dark eyes, radiating out to enfold her. He stroked her face and waited for her reply.

"Yes," she whispered, "*I will.*"

He kissed her again.

And time stood still.

Temia soared up to the clouds and felt certain that Jasper was looking down on her and smiling.

What he had told her through Mrs. Sebright had come true, even though she had not believed it.

Nestling in the Earl's sturdy chest, she felt as if they were already one.

Their love was so strong!

She could almost reach out and hold it.

It pulsated between them and bound them together.

"I did not believe we could ever be together," she sighed. "I felt our love was doomed."

"And I did not know if I could bear it to see you marry my best friend."

She put her fingers to his lips as if to silence him.

"Hush!" she whispered, "you must not have any recriminations. Our love has won through and Thomas will love again."

"He says not, but I know there is someone out there for him. Someone almost as wonderful as you!"

Temia smiled as he nuzzled her neck.

"I never dreamed I could be so happy! And now it has happened, I never want it to end."

The Earl moved back and looked at her.

His expression was serious and yet searching.

"It will never end, my darling," he said, with a voice full of emotion, kissing her shoulder as he spoke.

"God has blessed us with the greatest gift He can bestow. Love such as ours will last for ever."

"Yes," she sighed, as his lips met hers once more. "For ever!"